HIDDEN RICHES

13

TYNDALE HOUSE PUBLISHERS, INC., CAROL STREAM, ILLINOIS

RED ROCK MYSTERIES

#1 BEST-SELLING AUTHORS

ERRY B. JENKINS · CHRIS FABRY

Visit Tyndale's website for kids at www.tyndale.com/kids.

TYNDALE is a registered trademark of Tyndale House Publishers, Inc. The Tyndale Kids logo is a trademark of Tyndale House Publishers, Inc.

Hidden Riches

Designed by Jacqueline L. Nuñez

Edited by Lorie Popp

Published in association with Alive Literary Agency, 7680 Goddard Street, Suite 200, Colorado Springs, CO 80920. www.aliveliterary.com

For manufacturing information regarding this product, please call 1-800-323-9400.

Library of Congress Cataloging-in-Publication Data

Jenkins, Jerry B.
Hidden riches / Jerry B. Jenkins, Chris Fabry.
p. cm. — (Red Rock mysteries ; 13) (Tyndale kids)
Summary: While Bryce investigates who has framed their friend Boo for robbery, twin sister Ashley tries to find the previous owner of a painting, which had a map and a large amount of cash hidden in back.
ISBN 978-1-4143-0152-5 (sc)
[1. Crime—Fiction. 2. Christian life—Fiction. 3. Mystery and detective stories.] I. Fabry, Chris, date. II. Title. III. Series.
PZ7.J4138Hid 2006
[Fic]—dc22 2005036363

Printed in the United States of America

22 21 20 19 18 17 16
10 9 8 7 6 5 4

To Zach Blehm, faithful reader

"The past is never **Dead**.
It's not even past."

William Faulkner

"Birthdays are a **pain**. When you decide who you are going to invite, you've automatically not invited the rest of the world."

Marion Quidley

"We now have this **light** shining in our **hearts**, but we ourselves are like fragile clay jars containing this great treasure."

2 Corinthians 4:7

"Those who **fail** to remember the past don't get good grades in history."

Chuck Burly

PART 1

THE FIND

CHAPTER 1

Bryce

Sometimes big treasures are found in unlikely places. That's what happened to Ashley and me on a Sunday afternoon in November. She's my twin, born 57 seconds before me (which she always reminds me), and our birthday was less than two weeks away.

Sam, our stepdad, took us to our favorite thrift store in Colorado Springs while Mom worked on her latest book. She's an author and writes under the name Virginia Caldwell. Mom's eyes lit up when Sam offered to take our little brother, Dylan, too. Our older step-sister, Leigh, was out with her boyfriend, Randy, and that meant the house was going to be nice and quiet.

After we moved to Colorado from Chicago, Mom married Sam. Our real dad was killed in a plane crash caused by terrorists, and every birthday or holiday I think about what it would be like to get a present from him.

Dylan grabbed Sam's hand and dragged him into the store. If you've never been to a thrift store, you don't know what you're missing. Ashley likes clothes. She's found designer jeans in perfect shape for $4. I've found good hockey sticks and baseball gloves in great condition.

The store is laid out with racks of clothes in the middle and different sections running around the walls. Furniture is in the back, sports equipment is along the right wall, and the toy section is to the left.

You can figure out where Dylan and Sam went.

I had $10 saved up for Ashley's birthday present, and I slipped to a jewelry display. There were earrings, necklaces, and rings, but they all looked the same. I can't figure out why women like jewelry so much.

I was afraid Ashley was catching on, so I moseyed back to the sports section and found a $7 first-baseman's mitt.

Hmm. I had seen an earring-and-necklace set that was $3.50, and I distinctly remembered some change in the cup holder in Sam's truck.

That's when Ashley gasped. She has a distinct gasp—a cross between a rabbit just about to be picked up by a hawk and a bear discovering honey ham.

"Bryce, you've gotta see this!"

CHAPTER 2

❦ Ashley ❦

Some of my friends hate the thought of used clothes. If they only knew how many of my outfits came from these racks.

I thumbed through Christmas sweaters—snowflakes and Santas and reindeer—until I glanced at the back wall. Several pictures hung at eye level. Some had expensive golden frames. A velvet Elvis and several Ansel Adams black-and-white prints were propped against the wall.

But one painting took my breath away. I couldn't stop staring. I moved like a zombie toward it and called for Bryce.

A couple was standing near the picture, talking and pointing as I approached.

"That would go nice over the fireplace, don't you think?" the woman said. "It's so peaceful."

The man shook his head. "I want to put my dad's saber there. Maybe at the top of the hallway landing?"

The couple didn't notice me, even though I was standing right behind them. I stared over their shoulders.

The painting showed sheep grazing in a pasture near a stream so realistic you could almost hear water trickling over the rocks. Just the mountains rising behind the flock would have made the painting worth the $17.50 price. But it wasn't the sheep or the mountains or the stream or even the way the sky was painted that interested me.

"What is it?" Bryce said, making his way through the clothes.

The couple turned briefly and looked at us like we were ants at a picnic.

"Look at that," I said.

"Yeah, nice painting, but—" Bryce stopped, noticing what I had seen. "Whoa. That's incredible."

"Wouldn't Mom love it?" I said.

Bryce moved closer, studying the shepherd.

"We can find the right place when we get home," the woman said. "Let's get it."

The man turned. "Were you two interested in this?"

I nodded.

Bryce stepped forward. "The shepherd looks like someone we know."

I studied it again. The shepherd leaned against his staff and stared at the flock. You could see only the side of his face, but the resemblance was uncanny.

"He looks just like our dad," Bryce said.

CHAPTER 3

Bryce

"Your father?" the woman said. She was actually looking at us like we were humans instead of stains on a carpet. "Is he with you?"

"He passed away," Ashley said.

There was a long pause. Then the man held the picture up and winced. "Hon, looks like there's a scratch on the frame. I don't want a damaged picture, do you?"

She shook her head. "Better put it back."

The man handed me the picture. The wooden frame was huge, and it was a lot heavier than it looked. "We have to buy this," I said.

Ashley and I put our money together, which meant I had to give up on the first-baseman's mitt.

Then Sam walked toward us and looked at the picture. "Where you going to put that?"

"In Mom's office?" I said.

Dylan tugged on Sam with one hand and held a toy drum in the other. It looked like a toy Mom would put on a high shelf in his room. "Can we go now?"

Sam squeezed Dylan's hand and studied the painting. Clearly he didn't understand.

"It looks a lot like our dad—I mean, our first dad," Ashley said.

"Yeah, now I can see it," Sam said. "Your mother will love it."

I held the picture in front of me in the truck. When we went around a corner, it tipped and my knee went through the paper on the back.

When we got home, Ashley got some Goop from the laundry room, and we cleaned the frame. I tried to tape the hole in the back, but as I pressed, it ripped more. Ashley tried, but the hole got bigger. That's when I noticed something inside the frame. A piece of brown paper.

We tore some of the backing and used a screwdriver to pry a staple from the paper. It kind of looked like the Declaration of Independence or the Constitution, but when we opened it, we found a map.

"Bryce, this looks like a treasure map."

CHAPTER 4

⌘ Ashley ⌘

Everybody's heard stories about treasure maps. I took a deep breath as Bryce and I looked at markings and an *X* near a large tree. Behind the tree was a mountain with *D.P.* written on it.

"That has to be Devil's Paw," Bryce said.

Devil's Paw is a rock formation north of Red Rock. "But there's no way to tell how far away from the mountain it is," I said.

As Bryce studied the map, I tried to repair the rip. Something else caught my eye inside the painting. A blue zippered envelope sat at the bottom, fastened by staples. Bryce's jaw dropped when I ripped the paper all the way down. Then he saw the envelope, which was actually more of a pouch. He picked it up, and my heart thumped like Dylan's toy drum.

"I wonder how long that thing's been in there," I said.

"There's no date on the painting, but it sure looks old." Bryce unzipped the pouch.

CHAPTER 5

Bryce

Money. Lots of money. That's what I saw when I unzipped the pouch. Crisp bills. I picked up the first. Benjamin Franklin's face stared back at me.

$100.

I couldn't believe what I was seeing. I pulled the second bill out.

$100.

Benjamin Franklin was becoming a good friend. In all of American history I couldn't remember anyone I liked better than Benjamin Franklin.

Third bill.

$100.

Ben. My pal. Good buddy.

Fourth bill.

$100.

Ashley had a hand over her mouth. I pulled out a fistful of money and tossed it on my bed. There was nothing smaller than $100.

"Look at this!" Ashley said, half whispering, half screaming. It was a $1,000 bill.

My knees felt weak. The room spun, and visions of trips to islands and cruises danced through my head. Then I wondered how much those cruise boats cost—or a whole island.

"I've gotta tell Mom!" Ashley said.

I grabbed her wrist before she could fly out of the room. "Let's count it first."

"What do you mean, a bunch of money?" Sam said when we took the pouch to him.

"$37,400," Ashley said.

"We counted it three times," I said.

Sam's eyes opened as wide as the Grand Canyon. Then he smiled. "Looks real. What are you going to do with it?"

"It's ours?" I said. "I mean, can we legally keep it?"

"Keep what?" Leigh said, walking through the front door.

Ashley looked at me and rolled her eyes. I wanted to keep this a secret too. Leigh would probably want a percentage of the money.

"Bryce and Ashley found some money in an old picture," Sam said.

Leigh shrugged and headed upstairs. "Then they can buy their own Starbucks next time I take them."

"They could probably buy their own Starbucks *store* with this," Sam muttered.

Sam called Mom in, and we showed her the picture.

"We were thinking you'd like to put it in your office," I said.

It was one of those moments you anticipate. Would Mom see the resemblance?

She smiled and scanned the painting. Then she focused on the shepherd. "That looks like . . ."

"That's why we got it," Ashley said. "Doesn't it look like him?"

Mom held the picture, lost in the pasture scene. "It's amazing. The face looks . . ." A glint of water came to her eyes. "You know the psalm that talks about the valley of the shadow of death? Well, I've pictured your dad in heaven by a stream, enjoying God's company. Waiting for you two."

Mom looked at Sam and smiled. He's one of the nicest guys I know, but something's still holding him back from believing in God.

"There's something else they have to show you," Sam said, holding out the wad of bills.

CHAPTER 6

⌘ Ashley ⌘

Bryce reluctantly agreed to let me call the thrift store. I asked for the manager, and a nice lady said she was in charge.

"Do people ever find valuables in something they've bought? Like a painting that has money inside it?"

She chuckled. "No. A man found an old book worth a couple hundred dollars, but nobody's found any money that I know of."

"So what if somebody did find money?"

"If you bought it, it's your property." She paused. "Do you mind telling me how much?"

I told her.

She laughed and laughed. "I'll bet there's somebody who's not too happy they let that picture get away."

I thought about the couple who hadn't bought the painting. "Can I ask another question?"

"Sure, but it'll cost you." She laughed again, this time at her own joke.

"You send those big trucks out to pick up donations, right?"

"Yeah. And people use our drive-thru."

"Do you keep a record of where things come from? Is there any way to tell?"

Bryce gave me a look like he was going to rip the phone away.

"We don't keep records like that," the woman said. "Your painting could have come from anywhere in the area. Even Denver or Pueblo. If something doesn't sell in another store, we move it around until it does. I'm afraid you're stuck with that painting and the money."

CHAPTER 7

Bryce

I couldn't believe Ashley's questions, but when she told me what the woman had said, I felt better. I pulled out my watch calculator and punched in the numbers. "You and I both get $18,700."

"Bryce, we can't keep it."

I put a little finger in one ear and wiggled it. "Say that again. I could swear you just said we can't keep the money."

"We can't."

"Why not? We found it, didn't we?"

"Yes, but—"

"If somebody's dumb enough to put money inside an old painting and it winds up at the thrift store, I'm dumb enough to think it's mine."

"What if it was your painting? What if you were the one who put the money in there?"

"I wouldn't do that."

Ashley thought for a moment. "Remember our trip to the water park last year with Hayley? You left your wallet in their car."

"So?"

"Mrs. Henderson saw it and put it in a bag up front, and Mr. Henderson found it a few days later."

"I don't see what that—"

"You had $20 inside. What if Mr. Henderson had kept it? What if he said you shouldn't have left it lying around?"

"That's different. He knows us. We have no idea who—"

"Then let's find out whose money this is."

I shook my head. "I can't believe you're trying to mess this up. We could give a lot to the church. Or support missionaries. Or feed a village of . . . hungry villagers."

Ashley gave me one of her *yeah-right* stares.

"The person who owns this could be some drug dealer or thief."

"Or it could be a little old lady's savings that she hid because she was afraid her family would take all her money," Ashley shot back.

"So why'd the painting wind up in a thrift store?"

Ashley shrugged. "Maybe she died. Or maybe she got Alzheimer's and couldn't remember where she put it."

"Okay, let's say we look for the owner but fail. What then?"

"We split the money, and you can help those hungry villagers."

"How long are we gonna look?"

"Until we find them."

I rolled my eyes.

"Look, we have a map."

"We have squiggles on a page that could be anywhere within 50 miles of here."

Ashley grabbed the money and put it back in its zippered pouch. "Until we find the person, we should put this in Sam's safe so nobody can get it. And I don't think we should tell anyone at school."

CHAPTER 8

⌘ Ashley ⌘

I could tell that Bryce didn't like my idea. The truth was, my mind spun just as much as his about the cash and all I could buy.

Still, something inside said we'd regret it if we didn't try to find the owner. Part of me hoped we could keep the money, of course, but another part wanted to see the look on the person's face when he or she saw that zippered pouch. I couldn't imagine Jesus taking the money and slipping it into his pocket—if robes have pockets—or just handing it over to Judas, the treasurer.

I didn't sleep well that night. I kept thinking about all the ways to spend the money. Then another thought crept in. If thousands were in the painting, what secrets did the map hold? Gold? A million dollars?

I sat up, grabbed my journal and pen, and lit my candle. I go through a routine every time I write, and it works for me. I actually thought of how many candles and pens I could buy if we kept the money. I wrote:

> I have to tell myself the truth about this money. Sure, it could be fun to spend, but what if there's a widow out there looking for her lost coin and we're hanging on to it? God, help me do the right thing and not what's easiest.

I wrote my thoughts and feelings about the money, my family, school, my dance instructor, and our upcoming birthday party and sleepover.

Finally, my head drooped and I blew out the candle. Smoke rose in the moonlight, like swirling prayers lifting to the ceiling.

CHAPTER 9

Bryce

The next morning felt like a new year. Ashley and I were rich, and it had only cost $17.50. It made me wonder what else was at the thrift store.

I walked past Mom's office. She had hung the picture over her printer, replacing a poster of famous writers. I watched her type a little, then look back at the painting. It made me feel good to know she liked it enough to put it on her wall that fast.

Ashley looked like a zombie at the breakfast table. She had circles under her eyes and picked at her Corn Flakes.

"Change your mind yet?"

"About what?" she said.

"The money. We could look for years and never find—"

"That's not the point, Bryce. Aren't you curious?"

"Sure, but I'm more anxious to spend it."

She smiled. "We could split the money, and I'll look for the owner of my half."

I poured milk on my Honey Nut Cheerios, Corn Flakes, and Frosted Mini-Wheats and sighed. "If it were my money, I'd want someone to look for me. What's the first step?"

Ashley pulled out a list and handed it to me. "These are ideas I jotted down late last night."

1. Find out when the money was printed. Maybe this can narrow down the time the money was put into the picture or how long it's been there.
2. Take a picture of the picture. Go door to door near Devil's Paw and show it to people.
3. Look for more clues on the map. Maybe we're missing something.
4. Go to the police and see if anyone reported missing money. Maybe this is stolen.
5. DO NOT tell any of our friends about it. If they find out, they'll ask *us* for advances on their allowances.
6. Look through old newspapers for garage sales near Devil's Paw.

"I wish you'd be more detailed," I joked.

Ashley blushed. "I'm not saying we have to do all of that. I just couldn't sleep."

"I like them. Let's get started right after school."

PART 2

ACCUSED

CHAPTER 10

⌘ Ashley ⌘

It's hard to concentrate on class when you have $37,400 hanging on your mind like a backpack. Mrs. Sanchez called on me in first period, but I wasn't listening.

At lunch, my friends Marion Quidley and Hayley Henderson asked what was wrong.

"You've been spacey today," Hayley said.

"Just thinking about stuff at home," I said.

"Are your parents splitting?" Marion said. She's always looking for conspiracies about space aliens or global warming. She'd probably tell her next class that my parents were getting a divorce—on my birthday—and that Bryce and I were being sent to an orphanage for twins in Canada.

"No, nothing like that," I said.

"Is your mom going to have a baby?" Hayley said.

"What?"

"That would make me spacey," Marion said.

"My mom's not having more kids."

"Then what is it?" Marion said.

I took a bite of my apple and smiled.

My next class started uneventfully. We turned in an assignment at the start and watched a video. Pretty ho-hum stuff. Toward the end of class, a police car pulled into the parking lot. An officer got out, and a van pulled up. I craned my neck and noticed an insignia on the side. It was from Spring Hill, a juvenile detention facility.

A few minutes later, the intercom buzzed, and a secretary asked Aaron Heckler to the front office. Boo, as we call him, sat up and rubbed his eyes, like he'd slept through the video. He grabbed his books, but as he reached the door, the officer met him.

"What's going on?" Boo said.

"Come with us, Aaron," the officer said.

CHAPTER 11

Bryce

"You have to check on Boo," Ashley said when she found me in the hall. She explained what had happened in class and that he hadn't returned.

Caring what happens to the school bully may sound weird, but in the past few weeks, Ashley and I had gotten to know him better. He had actually helped out with one of our investigations. Plus, I had met his mother and talked with her in private. She asked me to be Boo's friend, and that hung over me like a dark cloud.

Being late to sixth period is like scheduling your own funeral, so I had to think fast. I'm a teacher's assistant for Mr. Gminski in first period, and he's also our speech coach. He had asked me to work on a flyer to encourage kids to try out for the team. I raced to his room and asked if he'd give me a late pass. "I want to start on the flyer early."

He squinted at me. "Now?"

"Mr. Gminski, it's really important, and I don't want to take advantage of you—"

"Fine," he said, handing me a hall pass. He wrote a note. "Make it quick. I only have so much pull with Mr. Bookman."

Mr. Bookman is our principal, and Ashley and I have had a few bad experiences with him.

I walked to the office and went to the corner that has a computer for teachers and their assistants. I logged on with Mr. Gminski's password and pulled up his notes. I studied the screen's reflection—the door to Mr. Bookman's office was closed, but it's made of glass. The shade was pulled down about halfway, and I saw a uniformed man just inside, blocking my view.

The secretary had a little radio tuned to a "light favorites" station, so I couldn't hear anything from inside until the announcer gave the weather.

"Why don't you tell us the truth?" a man said. I recognized the voice of Officer Ormsby, a man I'd met several times.

"It'll go much better for you if you admit the obvious, Aaron," Mr. Bookman said.

"I told you—I don't know what you're talking about."

"Then what about this?" the officer said. "We found it inside."

Some commercials played, and I lost the next few words.

The front door opened, and Boo's mother walked in clutching her purse.

"Hi, Mrs. Heckler," I said.

She glanced at me, then sighed. "Bryce. I'm glad you're here."

"What's going on?"

"They've accused Aaron. . . ." She teared up and her chin quivered. "The police came to our house and looked in his room. There had been a break-in overnight at—"

"Mrs. Heckler?" the secretary said. "You can go in now."

Boo's mom slowly walked inside. I had a good view and Boo turned. With emotion in his voice, Boo said, "Mom, you gotta believe me. I didn't do this!"

The secretary gave me a look.

I saved the information in the file and went to class.

He glanced at me, then [illegible]

"What's [illegible] her out?"

"[illegible] Asher [illegible]

[illegible] the [illegible] came to our [illegible]

[illegible]

[illegible] the [illegible]

[illegible]

[illegible]

[illegible]

CHAPTER 12

❀ Ashley ❀

My mind spun about Boo. I'd found out that his little sister had been killed, and I knew Boo felt responsible.

Our old principal, Mr. Forster, had taken an interest in him. He'd given Boo books and free smoothies at his business, Juicy Pages. With all the attention, Boo seemed like he was turning around.

I hurried to copy the homework assignment on the board as the bell rang, then rushed to the office. Bryce wasn't there, but the police car was still parked in front and Mr. Bookman's door was closed.

Marion Quidley walked past the office. "I heard Boo got caught again."

"Any idea what's going on?" I said. Marion has ideas about everything.

"I heard there was police activity at Red Rock Crossing this morning."

"Near the Toot Toot Café?"

"Yeah. It could be a rock through a window at one of the shops."

"I hope it's not the Toot Toot. Mr. and Mrs. Crumpus are the sweetest people in the world."

Bryce walked up, and Marion's eyes sparkled.

I told him what Marion had said.

Bryce shook his head. "I thought he'd changed."

"Boo?" Marion said. "Have you two been working your Christian voodoo on him or something?"

Bryce ignored her and said, "I talked with his mom briefly—"

"She's in there?" I said, biting my lip. "That's not good. That means he could be going back to Spring Hill."

"How do you know that?" Marion said. She seemed ticked that anyone would know more about something than her.

"I found out in my last class that the teachers got an e-mail about some police action against a student," Bryce said.

"If he goes back to Spring Hill . . ." I stopped just as the door to Mr. Bookman's office opened.

CHAPTER 13

Bryce

Officer Ormsby sat with Mrs. Heckler inside Mr. Bookman's office. Mrs. Heckler's back was to us, but I could tell by her body language that she was upset. She waved her hands and shook her head.

Kids filed past us like a human river, catching rides, unhooking bikes, and heading for home or after-school activities. Clouds had rolled in, and it looked like snow. Wind blew papers from backpacks, and kids screamed and chased them.

Ashley and I went to our lockers and returned. Finally a man came out of Mr. Bookman's office. He pulled the white van to the front of the building. Soon after, Mr. Bookman emerged, followed by the others. Boo was in the middle of the pack.

"He's not wearing handcuffs," Ashley whispered. "That's a good sign."

Mrs. Heckler had her arm around her son. Boo's eyes were red. He finally saw us and started to talk, but Officer Ormsby steered him toward the front door.

"Why are you taking him away?" Ashley said.

Mr. Bookman looked at us, his brow furrowed. "This is not your concern."

"We're his friends," Ashley said.

If you'd have told me a few months ago that those words would come from my sister's lips, I'd have thought you were crazy. But in a strange way, we *were* Boo's friends.

"My backpack," Boo said to the officer. "Can I take it with me?"

The officer nodded.

I followed them down the hall.

CHAPTER 14

❀ Ashley ❀

It was obvious that Mrs. Heckler cared about her son, but there was a lot of turmoil in her family—she and her husband weren't getting along. I wondered how she had tried to keep Boo out of trouble. A curfew?

"What's going on?" I whispered.

"It doesn't look good, Ashley," Mrs. Heckler said. "They're taking him back to Spring Hill."

"Why?"

"He knew one problem would send him back. The officer says they have strong evidence against him."

"About what?"

"A robbery at a dry cleaners."

There was only one at Red Rock Crossing—Carla's Cleaners. Mom takes her clothes there as well as some of Sam's shirts. It was just around the corner from the Toot Toot. "What did he take?"

"Money. And they say he vandalized the place. Because of the evidence, Aaron has to go back to detention."

"Do you think he did it?"

Mrs. Heckler crossed her arms. "He's never acted like he did in that office. I don't think he did it, but the police say they found the money in his room."

"Was he out last night?" I asked.

"Yes. He was gone until way after dark. He said he was meeting a friend."

Something troubled me in the woman's eyes, like she'd just had a terrifying vision.

"The thing that scares me most," she said, "is what might happen. Last time he came out of Spring Hill, he vowed he'd never go back. I don't know if he'll recover from another stay in that place."

CHAPTER 15

Bryce

Officer Ormsby walked ramrod straight, as if he were marching in a parade. He looked like Boo's shadow passing classrooms and lockers. It was weird seeing a guy with a gun in our school.

Boo reached his locker and flipped the tumbler. The locker didn't open, so he started over again, his hands shaking.

"You have something to say, Timberline?" Officer Ormsby said.

"Can I talk with Aaron?"

"Mr. Heckler is in custody, and I cannot give you permission to speak with him."

"Oh."

"However, my throat is somewhat parched, and I see a water fountain." He looked into Boo's open locker. "Get your things and be ready when I return."

"Yes, sir," Boo said.

It was the first time I'd ever heard Boo call anyone sir.

Officer Ormsby slowly walked to the water fountain.

"We don't have much time," I said. "What happened?"

"I went to see Ian Connor last night."

"Who's he?"

"He called and asked if I needed a part for the car I'm working on. I told him I needed a carburetor, and he said he had one. I went to the shops and hung around. He said he'd meet me there, but he didn't show until late, and then he didn't have the part."

"I'll bet you were ticked."

"Yeah, but I didn't break into a store and steal money." Boo's face was animated as he told the story, like he was dying for someone to believe him.

"Why do they think you did it?"

"They found money in my room. Do you think I'd be dumb enough to stash it in my bedroom?"

I didn't want to answer that question, so I just stood there looking at Officer Ormsby taking a long drink from the fountain. "Any other evidence?"

"My knife. It was used to pry open the cash register."

"How'd they know it was yours?"

"It had my name on it."

"Good reason."

"But I lost that knife. I haven't had it for at least a week."

"Where'd you lose it?"

"Don't remember."

"Is there anybody who wants revenge against you?" (I could think of only about a million people.)

Boo shrugged. "Just about everybody in this school."

"Yeah, but who would try to frame you for—?"

Boo pushed me against the locker. I'll never forget the look on his face. "You mean you believe me?"

I nodded. "This whole thing is too easy. It's like you're walking around with a big target on your back."

Officer Ormsby walked back, his boots clicking the tile.

"You and your sister are good at solving stuff," Boo said. "Will you help me?"

I nodded again. It was becoming a full-time job. "Here's what I want you to do. Write down everything about this. What you and Ian talked about. Who introduced you. If you've ever been in that dry cleaners. Where you lost your knife. People who might want to hurt you. Anything you can think of, write it down and get it to us."

His face fell. "They take most of our stuff away."

"Write it on toilet paper if you have to. Ashley and I will come to see you."

He looked up. "You mean it?"

You guessed it—I nodded. "But the quicker you write all that stuff down, the quicker we can get to the bottom of this."

Boo closed his locker and looked at it like it was the last time he'd ever see it. "I was just starting to like this school again."

CHAPTER 16

Ashley

Mrs. Heckler walked Boo to the van. It started sprinkling, and the cold drops felt like ice bullets. Kids gathered outside on their bikes. It would have been nice if Mr. Bookman had shooed them away, but he didn't. The kids laughed and whispered mean things about Boo.

Boo gave his mother a hug, and he broke down. It was like a dam bursting. "I don't want to go, Mama," he sobbed. "Please don't make me go back there."

His mom hugged him and whispered something. I don't care how much you don't like a person, seeing something like that makes you think twice. I wished everyone in school could see it.

Boo left and Mrs. Heckler thanked Bryce and me.

Officer Ormsby glared at the kids on bikes and told them, "Show's over. Go home."

We caught up with Officer Ormsby, and Bryce thanked him for letting him talk with Boo.

"I don't know why you're friends with that kid," the officer said. "He's nothing but trouble in my book."

"You actually found money at his house?" Bryce said.

"It's the easiest burglary we'll ever solve. He admits to being in the area. We talked with a friend of his who said he left him—"

"Ian Connor?" Bryce said.

"Yeah, that's him. We found Aaron's knife inside the store—half the blade was stuck in the cash-register door. Slam dunk."

"Doesn't he get a trial?" I said.

"He'll get a hearing, but they'll hold him at Spring Hill until that happens."

The rain came harder. "Doesn't it seem kind of weird that there's all that evidence? I mean, who would be so dumb as to leave a knife with his name on it at that shop?"

"Apparently Aaron would. You know he has a history."

"Didn't you hear him with his mom?" I said. "He didn't sound guilty."

"You ever been to Spring Hill? I'd cry if they were going to take me there." The officer started his car. "Look, you're good kids, but you're wasting your time. Heckler is guilty."

PART 3

INVESTIGATIONS

CHAPTER 17

Bryce

It was chilly and wet. Not a great day for a bike ride, but Ashley and I rode toward town. We were both freezing by the time we made it to Red Rock Crossing, so we parked our bikes outside the Toot Toot Café. Mr. Crumpus showed us to a booth, then came back a minute later with two mugs of hot chocolate and extra marshmallows. I think he has an inner sense of what people are going to order.

We told him about our family and how Mom's book was going. Then Ashley asked if he knew the owner of the dry-cleaning store.

Mr. Crumpus looked out the rain-splattered window at a sign. A sparkling shirt on a hanger hung above the words *Carla's Cleaners*. "Carla Sterling. Haven't had much contact with her, to be honest with you. Cars zoom in and out of there all the time, so they have a good business."

"Did you see police cars there this morning?" I said.

He nodded. "Guess somebody broke in overnight. It's funny though. We open here at six to serve breakfast. I saw Carla's car there at about 6:15, but I don't think the police got here until around nine."

"What time does she open?"

Mr. Crumpus scratched his head. "I think it's seven, so she can catch the going-to-work crowd."

"Why would she wait that long to report the break-in?" Ashley said. "Wouldn't she want the police to see the evidence?"

"You'd think so," Mr. Crumpus said.

I hovered over the hot chocolate, warming my face with the steam. "Has anybody ever had any trouble with Mrs. Sterling?"

"Miss," Mr. Crumpus said. "I hear she's had some problems with the young workers. Regular stuff. Not showing up for work on time. Haven't heard customers complain. What's this about?"

We told him, without revealing Boo's name.

"That's a shame. Kids who get in trouble at that age have a real problem digging out of the hole. Sometimes they never get over it."

CHAPTER 18

Ashley

Bryce and I stood outside Carla's Cleaners and watched a young woman help people. There were two registers, but the one to the right had police tape on it.

A middle-aged woman hung clothes on a metal bar at the front. She was thin, average height, with light brown hair. She turned and moved to the back. When the customers left, we walked into the hot room. It felt good, but I couldn't imagine it in summer.

"Welcome to Carla's—how can I help you?" the girl said. She seemed as excited about her work as I am about the latest hockey scores.

"We were hoping to talk with Miss Sterling," Bryce said.

"Carla?" the girl yelled.

Nice intercom, I thought.

"Yeah, what's up?" Carla said.

"We heard about the robbery," I said. "We go to the middle school—they just arrested the kid who did it. Thought you'd want to know."

She pursed her lips. "Well, I hate to see any young person get in trouble, but what are you gonna do?"

"A lot of people are probably glad to get rid of him," I said.

"Really? Shame to have a bad apple mess it up for everybody. This is a nice town."

I shook my head. "I bet you were shocked to find money missing this morning."

Carla nodded. "I actually didn't realize it at first because I had stuff to do in the back. Then I noticed the lock was jimmied, and that's when I found the register."

"Police sure solved it fast," Bryce said.

"Yeah, when they finally got here. I called them before we opened, but they didn't arrive for a couple of hours."

"Why would he break in here and not some electronics store or car-parts place?"

"Money is money, but I guess you'll have to ask him that. Now if you'll excuse me . . ." She went to the back.

Bryce and I left. It felt colder, but the rain had stopped. "Seemed like a nice lady," I said. "Cleared up the whole police thing."

"I'd still like to find out when the call came in to the station."

I wrote a note to ask Officer Ormsby about that. "You think Boo could be lying to us?"

"Didn't seem like it, but anything's possible." Bryce got on his bike. "I want to talk with this Ian Connor. You go back to the house and work on the painting stuff."

I laughed.

"What's so funny?"

"Nothing. It's just that for about a half hour, I forgot we were rich."

CHAPTER 19

Bryce

The talk with Miss Sterling bothered me. I'd hoped she would be some shifty-eyed weasel, but she'd answered our questions. My next hope was that Ian Connor would have something against Boo.

I rode to Juicy Pages, and Mr. Forster greeted me. I told him what had happened to Boo.

He clenched his teeth. "I was really hoping he was turning things around."

I borrowed his phone book, found two Connors, and hit the right number on the second try.

Ian's mother answered and said he wasn't home from work. "You can meet him here if you need to talk," she said. She told me where she lived, and I wrote down the directions. "What's this about?"

"A mutual friend, Aaron Heckler."

"All right," she said. "When he gets here, I'll tell him you're on your way."

Mr. Forster offered a fruit smoothie, but I told him I'd already had hot chocolate.

"I was thinking it might be a good idea to visit Aaron at Spring Hill," he said. "I know the director. Would you and Ashley want to go along if I can arrange it?"

"Absolutely," I said.

"I'll try to set it up for tomorrow."

Ian Connor's house was in the old section of Red Rock, his backyard ending at the railroad tracks. I wondered what it was like trying to sleep with trains rumbling all night. His mother invited me inside. She was older and had several cages of birds—cockatiels. She told me she sold them to make a little extra money.

"Ian should be here any minute," she said.

The squawking birds and the TV noise jumbled together to give me a headache. She put out some homemade chocolate-chip cookies, and they were the best I've ever tasted.

"Where does Ian work?"

"At his uncle's business, Mile High Disposal."

A junkyard, I thought.

"He's worked there ever since he graduated from high school," she continued.

"How long ago was that?"

"Last spring. I want to send him to college, but unless I start raising geese that lay golden eggs, he'll have to work a few years. He's also talked about going into the military because they help pay for college."

"Do you know Aaron Heckler?" I said.

"Is that one of Ian's friends? Name doesn't sound familiar."

I waited long enough for the sun to go down and the temperature to drop 10 degrees. I had a long ride home, but I wanted to talk with this guy.

The phone rang, and Mrs. Connor answered. "All right, honey, I'll tell him."

"Was that Ian?" I said after she hung up.

She nodded. "He's really sorry. He said he had a flat tire coming home and had to get it fixed."

I nodded. "I'll try to catch him later. Thanks for the cookies."

CHAPTER 20

❋ Ashley ❋

It was hard to think about money after seeing Boo's scene. I wanted to stay with Bryce, but I had homework *and* a map to investigate.

At dinner, I told Mom that Bryce was still out, and she seemed to be in her own world. That happens a lot when she's in the middle of a book. She'll get a far-off look and then write something on her computer. "Have you decided who you're inviting to your birthday party?" she said.

"I want to invite Ruth from the youth group, but I'm not sure how she'll mix with Marion and Hayley."

"Mix how?" Sam said.

It's hard to talk about spiritual things when Leigh's around because she's negative about God. Sam isn't a Christian either, but he's able to talk about that kind of stuff.

"Well, Ruth can be mean to people who don't go to church. I've been trying to talk with Marion and Hayley about important stuff for months, and Ruth could ruin all I've worked for."

"Invite someone else," Sam said.

"But I really want Ruth."

"Could you talk with her ahead of time?" Mom said. "Explain?"

"You don't think that would offend her?" I said.

"You're just being honest," she said. "I'm sure she can handle it."

Bryce finally came home, frowning. I figured he'd struck out with Ian.

Before I called Ruth, I borrowed Mom's digital camera, took a couple shots of the painting, and printed them. I also loaded them onto our computer. Maybe there was someone I could e-mail the shots to who might know where the painting came from.

CHAPTER 21

Bryce

I scarfed down dinner as fast as I could. There was a lot to do. I called the police department, and the guy at the desk said Officer Ormsby was gone. I left a message.

Then I wrote down a bunch of questions and took a deep breath. Sometimes talking on the phone makes me nervous, like I'm going to start stuttering again, but preparation takes some of the fear away. I dialed Ian's house.

"Hullo?" The voice was deep and kind of twangy.

"Ian? My name is Bryce."

"Oh yeah, sorry I didn't make it home. What did you need?"

"I'm checking on the Aaron Heckler deal."

"You with the school newspaper or something?"

I could have easily said yes, but that would have been lying. Ashley and I have an unwritten rule that we won't lie to someone to get information. Sometimes we've crossed the line, and both of us have felt bad about it.

"No, Aaron's just a friend."

"Really?" He said it like I had told him my mother is a werewolf.

"Aaron said he met you last night to get some kind of car part?" I said.

"Yeah, he needed a carburetor. I took one from a car at my uncle's place, but it turned out to be a different model."

"Why didn't you call him and tell him you had the wrong one?"

"I didn't realize it until I got there. It took me a long time to get the thing out of the engine. Believe me, I was just as upset as Heckler."

"He was upset?" I said.

"Yeah, said there was no way he'd get the car started. He didn't have money for a new one, and his parents wouldn't lend it to him. He picked up a rock and tossed it halfway to Kansas. I was afraid he'd break a window."

"Did you see him leave the parking lot?"

"No. Last I saw him, he was walking to the back of the shops."

"That's how the thief got in, through the back door," I said.

Beep.

Call-waiting sounded, and I looked at the readout. It said *Red Rock Police Department.* "Can you hang on a second, Ian?"

"Sure."

I pushed the Flash button and spoke with Officer Ormsby. "How can I help you, Bryce?"

"This morning when you went to the cleaners, did you go right away or was there a delay?"

"We had an accident up on Ram's Horn Hill about the time Miss Sterling called. A truck pulling a horse trailer flipped. I'd say I didn't get over to the cleaners for maybe two hours."

"That's what she told me."

"You still think this Heckler kid is innocent?"

"I'm not sure. Can I ask you something else?"

"Sure."

"Have you heard anything about anyone missing some money? Especially people north of us, near Devil's Paw?"

He hesitated. "Is there something you want to tell me?"

"No, I'm just wondering."

"I haven't heard any reports."

"Okay, one more thing. Was the horse hurt?" I figured that was the first question Ashley would ask me.

"No, the trailer was empty. Driver was banged up and had to go to the hospital though."

When Ian came back on the line, I asked him straight-out, "Do you think Aaron broke into the cleaners?"

"Well, I heard they found his knife in there, and he was headed toward the back of the building. Who else could it be?"

"One more question. How did you know he needed a carburetor?"

"Friend of his mentioned it. Why?"

"Who?"

He paused. "I think I'm done answering questions."

Click.

CHAPTER 22

✾ Ashley ✾

I called Ruth, and Mom drove me there because it was dark. Bryce and I call Ruth's place the Gingerbread House because it looks like the witch's house in Hansel and Gretel. The front is red brick with lights along the driveway.

Ruth and I went downstairs to the family room. There were all kinds of DVDs on a shelf, along with some popular Christian books and a few Bibles. I noticed they didn't have any of my mom's books.

Ruth has two sisters, Naomi and Elizabeth, and I was glad she didn't have brothers because they'd probably be named Boaz or Mephibosheth. I told Ruth about my party, and she squealed with delight. "I was hoping you'd invite me this year!"

I took a deep breath. "I wanted to talk to you about the others who will be there. I don't think you know them. Hayley and Marion. They go to my school."

She closed her eyes in thought. "Hasn't Hayley come to youth group? Blonde hair? Big eyes?"

"Yeah, that's her."

"Well, if you're doing this as an outreach, I totally understand. I went through the evangelism class last spring. They usually don't let kids go through it, but the pastor said I was advanced for my age, so I know exactly what to do."

I scooted back, and the leather couch screeched. "Well, I actually didn't want it to be a Bible study or anything. I think I just want to have fun with everybody."

"I get it. Pre-evangelism. We learned about that in the class. You invite them to some social event, a cookout, whatever, and then the next time they come over, POW! You hit them with the gospel. Great idea."

I reached for my soda and took a sip. "That's not really the plan either."

Ruth sat forward, her brow furrowed. "Ashley, you're not ashamed of the gospel, are you? Because if that's it, I think you're letting God down."

I put the soda down. This was what I feared most. "I want to be their friend whether they believe what I believe or not. They already know how I feel about God and Jesus. I think the more they see me live what I believe, the more interested they'll get. Marion is really smart—"

Ruth quoted a verse about the foolishness of the cross and how God hates human wisdom. I was beginning to regret inviting her.

"Here's the thing," I said. "I just want to have a fun party. I don't want Marion or Hayley to feel awkward by asking them to pray or writing John 3:16 on my cake. Who knows, they may want to talk about spiritual things, and that'll be great. But if they don't, that's okay too."

Ruth sat back and looked away. "I'm sorry to hear that, Ashley. Tell your mom I can't come to the party." She stood and walked out of the room.

CHAPTER 23

Bryce

In class the next day, I overheard some kids talking about Boo. One said he'd trashed the store, torn up clothes, and ruined a machine. Another said he had tied up the cashier and threatened her. There's a time to stick up for friends and a time to just listen.

"I heard they took him to Spring Hill in handcuffs," another said, "and when he wouldn't cooperate, they shoved him into the van and made his mouth bleed. Broke his nose."

"We won't be hearing from Boo for a long time. I heard they put him in solitary."

"Suits me. That way he can't beat us up."

At lunch, I called Mr. Forster. He'd set up a meeting at Spring Hill at 4:30. "We'll leave from Juicy Pages after you get out of school, if that's okay with your parents."

Our English teacher gave us an assignment to work on overnight. "I want you to have fun with this, but watch your grammar."

"My grammar died last year," Duncan Swift said.

Everybody laughed.

"Cute," Mrs. Ferguson said. "Now here's the assignment. What would you do if you found a million dollars? How would you spend it? Would you give any of it away? Who would you give it to? Would you save any of it?"

She asked us about a hundred questions, but I wasn't listening. I was thinking about the $37,400 sitting back at our house.

CHAPTER 24

Ashley

I got a pass and went to the library during my last class. I used a computer and logged on to the Spring Hill Web site. The pictures made it look like a modern retreat, better than any beachfront vacation. All the rooms were well lit, the carpet was bright, and every room sparkled.

But I'd heard stories from people who knew better—and not just Marion Quidley. Every kid who had a visitor had to go through a strip search. I don't even like changing clothes for gym class.

We met Mr. Forster at Juicy Pages and parked our bikes in the back. He had a small cooler with him but didn't tell us what was in it.

After he asked how school had gone and what we thought of Mr. Bookman, the new principal, we didn't say much. The smooth-jazz station he chose made me want to sleep.

We passed the Air Force Academy and its football stadium. A few minutes later we took an exit that went straight through downtown Colorado Springs and headed east. We passed businesses, statues, landmarks, and row after row of houses, and then we hit a stretch of wilderness. It was like civilization ended.

As we drove, I couldn't stop thinking about the party and what Ruth had said. Was I ashamed of God? Was I scared of what my friends thought of me?

It was almost 4:30 when Mr. Forster pointed. "There it is."

The building was surrounded by a fence higher than a basketball hoop. (I knew that because there were four basketball hoops inside the fence.) Sharp wire at the top of the fence looped around it like a ring. The building itself was square and had several levels. It almost looked like a school if you took away the guard post in front and all the No Trespassing signs.

The guard looked at his clipboard and said we were approved. He told us where to park, then looked at Bryce and me. "What's the nature of your visit?"

"We have a friend here."

The man nodded slightly. "Hope he or she has a short stay. Go on in."

PART 4

SPRING HILL

CHAPTER 25

Bryce

The first thing I noticed inside was the alcohol smell. I've been in hospitals that didn't look this clean. We walked down a long hallway and through a heavy locked door. Beyond that was the metal detector, and we had to empty our pockets. A guard named Steve checked us out and waved us through.

Mr. Forster's friend showed us some cells, which were basically rooms with two beds, two desks, and a toilet. "This is the pod for the puma section. We give each block an animal name to keep it straight. Our students can come here to study or just socialize."

He said "students" but he really meant "inmates." There wasn't a kid here who wanted to be.

We walked through another door and down another hallway with several empty rooms. "Just have a seat. I'll get Aaron," the man said.

"Where is he?" I said.

"Class. This is a regular school. We like to keep the mind engaged as much as possible."

"Are there kids here who won't get out?"

He nodded. "Some pretty rough ones. The things you read about in the newspaper—the assaults by teenagers, shootings, burglaries. . . . There's a kid here who didn't want his stepmother nagging him about homework. The stepmother's gone. Another kid went camping with a friend. The friend never came back." He pointed to the pod as several kids walked to their rooms. "Some sell drugs. Others are petty burglars. Unless they're tried as an adult, they're sent here."

"Do any change?" Ashley said. "I mean, are you ever able to help them turn their lives around?"

"That's why I'm here. I believe each kid deserves a chance. They have a choice. We're here to show them there's a way out if they want to make that choice."

The man excused himself, and Mr. Forster sat. Ashley and I watched several guys in blue outfits. Behind them was a guard with massive arms. It was the faces of the kids that struck me. They looked hopeless, abandoned.

I thought about things I'd been accused of doing and wondered how long I'd survive in here.

CHAPTER 26

❀ Ashley ❀

There were several posters on the walls, including a lake with an inspiring quote. Another showed a guy climbing an icy mountain, his face filled with determination. Instead of a list of rules like No stabbing or No drug dealing, there was a picture of a cat curled up in a ball. *Contentment,* it said.

Boo walked into the room, his head down. He wasn't shackled, but it looked like someone had handcuffed his heart. When he saw Mr. Forster and the smoothie he'd brought in the cooler, he looked away, like it reminded him too much of his old life. He finally sat down, took the drink, and stirred it.

"I brought you a book too," Mr. Forster said. "You liked one of the other titles this author wrote."

"Thanks. From what they say, I'll have time to read it."

"Has your mom been here?" I said.

"Yeah, she came earlier with a lawyer. Not the one we had before—he had something better to do, I guess. I don't think this new one believed a thing I said."

"Bryce and Ashley told me your story," Mr. Forster said. "They want to help you prove your innocence."

Boo nodded and pulled a memo pad from his pocket. "I wrote a bunch last night. Everything I could remember."

Bryce flipped through the pad. "This'll be a good start. I talked to Ian Connor."

Boo sat up. "What did he say?"

"He didn't know he had the wrong part, and you were mad. When he drove away you were headed for the back of the building."

Boo nodded. "That's the quickest way to get home."

"Did you notice anybody back there? anything strange?"

Boo shook his head. "There's a light by the door and some trash cans. I didn't see anybody."

"We also talked with the store owner, Miss Sterling," I said. "Have you ever been in there? Would she want to hurt you?"

Boo looked away. "I only set foot in that place one time, and that was because I thought it was the dollar store. When I saw all those clothes and felt how hot it was, I turned around. I wouldn't recognize that lady if she walked in here right now."

"What about the knife?" I said. "Remember where you lost it?"

Boo thought a minute. "Yeah. I remembered last night, but I don't know if it's important."

"Let us be the judge of that," I said.

CHAPTER 27

Bryce

Boo grabbed a pen and opened the small, spiral-bound notebook. "This is my house right here. Sometimes when there's nothing to do and the weather's okay, I go fishing at this pond in the woods."

"The reservoir?" I said.

"Nah, there's too many people there. This ridge takes you to a big rock cliff and a grove of aspen trees. The lake is there."

"I've never heard of it," Ashley said.

"That's probably because it says Keep Out and No Trespassing and that kind of stuff all over the place."

"Do you know whose property it is?" I said.

"I thought the lake was public land, but maybe not." He bent over the pad and drew a path through the woods behind his house. "On this side of the mountain is a trail. You can get there with four-wheelers."

"How do you know that?" I said.

"I've seen them up there."

"Why didn't you take that path?" Mr. Forster said.

"The way I go is shorter."

I examined the drawing. "If you're here, can you see Kangaroo Rock?"

"No, it's blocked by lots of trees, but if they weren't there you could see it."

"Where did you lose the knife?" Ashley said.

Boo sighed, like a big confession was coming. "There are some rocks here—that's the best part of the lake to fish. I had my line in the water and was cleaning a nice rainbow trout when I heard the four-wheelers. I kinda hunkered down so they wouldn't see me. So these ATVs come to the back part of the lake. They had a couple of barrels strapped on."

"Did you see the drivers?" I said.

"They had helmets and goggles. Gloves. Big plastic coats. Couldn't see their faces."

"What happened next?" Ashley said.

"Well, they drove up the trail behind the lake. Then they got off and unstrapped the barrels. That's when it happened."

"What?" I said.

"I got a big strike on my rod. I'd wedged it in between a couple of rocks, and the rod bent like crazy."

"What'd you do?" Ashley said.

"I couldn't let the fish get away, so I reeled it in. The fish kind of jumped and splashed, and those people saw me. They yelled and started their ATVs. I knew it was time to get out of there."

"And you left your knife?"

Boo nodded. "I took my rod but forgot the knife. I ran down the hill, through the aspen trees where I knew the ATVs probably wouldn't follow. But they did. I hid until they zoomed down the hill."

"You didn't see their faces?" Mr. Forster said. "Hear their voices?"

"No, the engines were too loud, and the helmets covered their faces."

"Is that the only knife you had with your name on it?" Ashley said.

Boo nodded. "My dad gave it to me."

CHAPTER 28

Ashley

"Any idea what was in those barrels?" I said.

Boo shrugged. "At first, I thought it was fish. You know, stocking the lake. But they took the barrels up to where the stream forks."

"What stream?" Bryce said.

"Right here above the lake, there's a mountain stream that runs most of the year. It forks off and a little runs into the pond, but most of it runs on the other side of this ridge."

We asked Boo a few more questions, but he was out of answers.

Mr. Forster put a hand on Boo's shoulder. "Your friends and I are going to do everything we can to help you. You believe that?"

Boo's eyes welled with tears. "Yeah."

Mr. Forster pushed the buzzer. Bryce and I said stuff like, "Hang in there" and "Don't let this place get you down," but the look on Boo's face said we didn't know anything.

Before Boo left, he turned to me. "Has Mrs. Sanchez heard anything about her mother?"

The question caught me off guard. Mrs. Sanchez had told us days ago that her mom was ill, but I thought Boo slept through class.

"Yeah, the tests came back negative. It's good news."

Boo nodded and walked through the door.

I asked Mr. Forster why they had to search him, and he said some people try to smuggle stuff inside. It seemed Boo was being treated like an animal.

As we drove home, Mr. Forster said, "What do you think of his story? He could be making all this up."

Bryce winced. "I'd like to go up to that lake and check it out."

"But who would want to send Aaron away?" I said.

Bryce handed me the memo pad. "Maybe there's a clue in here."

As Mr. Forster drove, I opened the pad and looked at Boo's scrawled handwriting. There were names, then a dash, then what Boo had done to the person.

Redheaded freckled kid who rides the bus—I shoved him into the mud before school last year, Boo had written. *I don't think he's forgotten it.*

Boo looked like an equal-opportunity bully. There were as many girls' names in the pad as there were boys'. I had to admit there were lots of people who were mad at him, but mad enough to steal money to send him to Spring Hill?

Toward the back, Boo had written something and crossed it out. I strained to see it and finally made it out.

I feel bad about my dad leaving. Part of it feels like it's my fault. If I had been better, maybe he and Mom wouldn't be separated.

That hit me right in the heart. Boo felt his parents' marriage trouble was because of him.

The rest of the ride home was a blur. I closed the memo pad. All I could do was pray for Boo, his parents, and that we could find out the truth, no matter who got hurt by it.

PART 5

SEARCHING FOR CLUES

CHAPTER 29

Bryce

I had a hard time sleeping that night, thinking of Boo in the puma pod, lying in his cell. The moon seemed like a white cyclops staring at me, and I wondered if Boo could see it.

I studied the memo pad. He'd written that he had tried hard not to do anything bad during Halloween. Ashley and I had seen him that night.

The next morning, Ashley and I agreed that we'd split up the investigations. I would take the lead on Boo, and she would follow up on the painting. She asked Sam if she could take a couple of the bills to have them analyzed. I could tell by the look on his face that he thought it was a bad idea.

"I don't know if you should be carrying around that much cash," he said.

I figured he was thinking of all the money we'd lost. We'd leave some in a jacket pocket and misplace it, a wallet would fall out, or we just wouldn't be able to find it.

"Why don't you come back here after school?" Sam said. "I'll leave a couple of the bills with your mom."

Ashley smiled. "Sounds like a plan."

At school I followed up with every kid Boo had written about. Most of them were younger, shorter, and thinner than Boo. Of course, just about everyone was smaller than him since he's older than us. Each one denied having anything to do with sending him away, and each said they were glad he was gone. I believed them.

The last kid I talked to was the redheaded kid who had been pushed into the mud. He was a seventh grader with long, gangly arms and a face to match. His hair was bright red and seemed to swirl on his head like one of those cinnamon rolls they make at the Black Bear Bakery.

"You know Aaron Heckler, right?" I said as the kid moved toward his bus.

He looked at me like I had six heads. "Who doesn't?"

"You know he was arrested for a break-in a couple of days ago."

A few kids pushed past us. "I heard. What's this got to do—?"

"He told me he pushed you into the mud. That you might be so ticked off that you'd do something to hurt him."

The boy grinned. "He's scared of *me*? He thinks I would do that?"

"Were you involved? Or maybe you know somebody who was."

He laughed, and it wasn't because he thought the whole thing was funny. "You think he's innocent? Are you that desperate for a mystery that you'd believe Boo Heckler?"

The kid had obviously heard about Ashley and me. Though we'd tried to keep our investigations quiet, word had spread over the past few months.

"Give it up, Timberline," the kid said. "Stop trying to solve a riddle that's already been solved."

I'm not trying to be mean, but if there had been a mud puddle nearby, I think I'd have pushed him in myself.

CHAPTER 30

❀ Ashley ❀

I rode my bike home as fast as I could. Mom had the envelope with money ready. I fired up the ATV and slammed on my helmet. You might think November in Colorado is cold, but it can be really warm. Fortunately this was a warm day.

I parked at Mrs. Watson's house, a family friend, and walked into town. I'd called Johnny's Pawn and Deli at lunch, and he'd told me he could help.

Johnny was behind the counter. He's a huge man who looks like he belongs on a motorcycle. Leather jacket. Ponytail. The pawnshop sold a lot of interesting things at high prices. There were TVs, DVD players, guns, knives, guitars, and even a drum set. Johnny also had rare coins in a glass case, along with various baseball and football cards. He'd helped Bryce and me out before, but I'm not sure he recognized me. Probably every pawnshop owner looks at kids as nuisances, unless they have a lot of money with them, which I did.

"I deal more with gold and silver coins than I do with currency, but I should be able to help you," Johnny said. He had kind of a high-pitched voice for such a big man.

He put a magnifying glass on the $100 bill and showed me the 1934 on the front. He told me something about the secretary of state and how you could check the signature and a bunch of other stuff I didn't catch. It was kind of hard to understand, like a doctor explaining brain surgery.

I chuckled and gave him my million-dollar smile. "So, what does all that mean?"

"Well, this is definitely younger than 1934—if you want to put it that way. I'd say it was printed in the late '40s. Maybe early '50s." He took out the $1,000 bill and whistled. "Haven't seen one of these in a long time."

"Why not?"

"They actually stopped making them. You want to tell me what this is about?"

"I'm looking for the owner of these," I said, reaching for the $1,000.

He held on to it and grinned. "You could buy a lot of things in here. Nice jewelry. Maybe a watch?"

"It's not mine," I said.

He let go, and I tucked the bills away and shoved the envelope deep into my pocket.

Johnny sighed. "The $1,000 bill is still circulating. I can't pinpoint when they might have gotten this. Could have been 50 years ago, could have been a month ago."

I thanked him and hurried to my ATV. I kept looking over my shoulder, hearing footsteps that weren't there.

By the time I got to the ATV, I was running. Night was coming on faster and faster the closer we got to December. I turned my headlight on and zipped toward the pasture near our house.

CHAPTER 31

Bryce

After school I rode my bike past Ian's house. I thought about riding to the dump, but it's a long ride with lots of hills. I saw Mr. Forster in the window of Juicy Pages, and he waved me inside. He seemed glad to see me and made a mug of hot chocolate—one of the advantages of living in a small town where everybody knows you.

"How's the investigation?" he asked.

"Lots of dead ends."

"You hear anything from Aaron's mom?"

I shook my head.

"I may have something that will interest you." Mr. Forster moved to the cash register and pulled out a folded map. "I checked that lake Aaron talked about and came up with some good news."

The map was old, wrinkled, and had squiggly lines all over it. "This shows the elevation of the area and some of the natural landmarks regular maps don't." He pointed to an area with a blue spot on it. "Now if I'm right, this is the lake."

"Does it have a name?" I said.

"A forest ranger I called said everyone knows it as Hidden Lake."

"That fits."

"These areas are private, but this patch of land, plus this trail here, is public."

"So he didn't have to trespass to get there."

"Right. If he'd have taken this trail, which starts here, there'd be no problem."

CHAPTER 32

❀ Ashley ❀

After dinner Bryce told me about the lake, and we agreed to drive there on the weekend. I told Bryce what I'd learned about the money—which wasn't much.

"So the map is our best clue," Bryce said.

"I searched newspapers on the Internet and didn't find any articles on stolen money or missing cash."

"Did you try garage sales?"

"The papers I saw don't keep classifieds like that online."

"So we're back to square one."

"Maybe we should look at the map one more time," I said.

Bryce brought it to the bright light in the kitchen, where we do our homework. He held the map up to the light to see if there was a watermark—something that might make the paper unusual. Nothing. It was just a plain sheet of paper.

We both hovered over the page and stared. "You choose who you're going to invite to your party?" I said.

"Duncan, Chuck, and Kael."

He said it like it didn't take him two seconds to decide. I'd agonized for weeks. "Are all three coming?"

"Yep. Asked them today. Who are you inviting?"

I told him what had happened with Ruth and gave him the rest of the list.

"Marion Quidley? Are you nuts?"

"She's nice, and besides, she has a big crush on you. I'll probably let her go through your room and pick out a souvenir."

Bryce stood straight. "You do and I'll tell Duncan you've got a thing for him."

"You wouldn't!"

"Hey, what's going on?" Leigh said. She walks in at some of the worst moments. Bryce and I were so engrossed in our argument that we forgot about the map. "What's this?" she said, picking it up.

"Just something we found in that old painting," I said.

Leigh looked at me. "Your mom said you guys found money. How much?"

"Enough to make us wonder who it belongs to," I said.

She stared at me. "You're not going to keep it? If I bought some old picture and found money inside, I wouldn't waste time looking for the owner. I'd spend it."

I know you would, I thought.

"It's one of our silly little mysteries," Bryce said. Leigh acts like we're stupid kids with toy binoculars.

"How are you going to find out whose it is?" she said, studying the map.

"We think it's somewhere near Devil's Paw, but so far we've struck out."

Leigh scratched her chin. "If you offer me enough for gas money, I'll give you a ride up there."

"What's the catch?" Bryce said.

"Wait a minute," I said. "Did Mom put you up to this?"

She smiled. "Here's the deal. If you don't find out whose money it is, I get a percentage. Let's say 20 percent. If you do find them, I don't get anything."

"You don't even know how much it is," Bryce said.

Leigh couldn't hide her smile any more than a skunk could hide his stink. Mom had told her how much we'd found.

"If you get a reward, I'll take 20 percent. Either way, you each get 40 percent."

I looked at Bryce. He shrugged. "This way we won't have to bug Mom or Sam."

"Make it 15 percent," I said.

"Deal," Leigh said.

CHAPTER 33

Bryce

After school on Thursday I rode bikes with Kael toward Boo's house. We talked about the party, now less than a week away.

"My mom wants to know what you want," Kael said.

I didn't have the heart to tell him I was rich beyond my dreams, so I gave him a couple of DVD choices and added that I always like Chicago Cubs shirts and hats. "Whatever is fine."

"Who's your sister inviting?"

I told him. "We'll stay in the barn—where Sam's office is. He said we could take an extra TV out and play games and watch videos."

"We gonna scare the girls?"

I shrugged. "We'll see."

We reached a turnoff, and I headed down the dirt road to Boo's house. The road had deep ruts, and my tires turned red from the clay.

I parked in their driveway, and Jessie, Boo's little sister, came out. She held some plastic horses to her chest, and it made me think of all the times Ashley and I used to play with toys like that. Jessie put them on the porch and arranged them in a circle, ignoring me.

Mrs. Heckler walked out, drying her hands. She had worry written all over her face. "What a nice surprise. Come in. Aaron told me that you saw him yesterday."

"So you've talked to him? How's he doing?"

We went into the kitchen, and she handed me a blueberry muffin. The whole house smelled like a bakery. "It's hot," she said.

I let it cool in front of me, taking in the delicious smell.

"He's not too well," she said. "There was a boy he knew from the summer who attacked him last night on the basketball court. I guess they'd argued before."

A bully getting attacked by another bully—normally my idea of justice. "Is he okay?"

"Physically he's fine. He sounded really tired, though." Mrs. Heckler took a deep breath. "There's something else." She ran her hand across the tablecloth. "I talked with one of our neighbors who didn't know what happened. She said she saw Aaron walking by her house the night of the robbery. He was carrying something, Bryce."

Mrs. Heckler put a hand to her forehead. "All this time I've thought . . . well, I'm beginning to think the police are right."

I ate the muffin in three bites and tossed the paper in the trash. "Do you mind if I take a look in his room?"

CHAPTER 34

❀ Ashley ❀

Mom asked me to watch Dylan while she ran a few errands. I took my homework to his room and let him play with his car collection. He has a carpet he rolls out that has roads, gas stations, supermarkets, and parking lots painted on it. He's in his own world with his Matchbox cars and that carpet.

Pippin and Frodo wandered upstairs and lay down at my feet. Usually Frodo isn't allowed up here but he looked so cute, I let him stay. Pippin is old now and walks slower, but Frodo chases him and nips at his shaggy ears and tail.

The doorbell rang and I answered it. I expected some kid selling magazines or popcorn or candles or entertainment books. Instead, it was Ruth and her mother.

"May we come in?" Ruth's mother said.

"Sure."

I opened the door wide, and they stepped inside. I told them nobody was home except Dylan and me.

"I'd hoped to catch your mother." She cleared her throat. "Ruth has talked to me about your party. She'd like to come if the invitation is still open."

Why couldn't Ruth tell me this herself? I wondered. "Great," I said.

"I just wanted to make sure you won't be mixing with the boys. I assume Bryce will have some of his friends."

I explained that we'd be in the house, and they would be in the barn.

Ruth just studied the tile in our entry.

"I see. And the other two girls are . . . ?" her mom said.

"My friends from school."

"Mmm-hmm. Ruth and I have talked about people having different approaches to those . . . outside the faith. Your parents send you to a public school, and I respect that. Your mother is in a tough position, living in a divided home."

She was talking about Sam not being a Christian. A lot of people don't understand that she became a Christian *after* she was married.

"You think she should leave Sam?" I said.

"No, I admire your mother. I'm just saying it's difficult. For her and you."

I didn't want to be snippy, but I had to say something. "I love my stepdad whether he believes like I do or not. I pray for him every day, and I hope you will too. But I don't think Jesus would abandon him just because—"

"Of course not," she said. "We certainly will pray. Is there anything you would like for your birthday?"

Dylan's cars clattered upstairs.

I mentioned a couple of books I wanted. Sometimes you wonder if you've made the right choice for your party. I had the sinking feeling something bad was about to happen.

CHAPTER 35

Bryce

For the second time in my life, I walked into Boo Heckler's room. Boo's bed was made, and there were no clothes on the floor—his mom had definitely been in here. The smell of lemon-scented furniture polish hung in the room.

"What are you looking for?" Mrs. Heckler said.

"Where did they find the bag of money?"

She pointed. "There, right underneath the mattress."

I picked up the mattress and looked; then I studied the room. "You were gone that afternoon before the robbery, right?"

"Yes, I had errands to run."

"Do you lock your doors when you go out?"

"I didn't until recently when my husband moved . . . yes. The house was locked."

"Did you notice any open windows?"

"The only one who keeps the window open is Aaron," she said. "It can be 40 degrees below zero, and he'll have the window cracked and be sleeping on top of his covers."

I looked at Boo's window. "Did you lock this when you cleaned in here?"

She put a hand to her chin. "As a matter of fact, yes. It was unlocked."

I pulled the lock back and lifted the window. The screen had four tiny pins that held it in the wooden frame. There was a hole in the screen near the bottom two pins. "Do you know how this hole was made?"

She studied it. "Not unless Aaron leaned against it or something. We had all of our screens repaired this past summer."

I went outside and checked the ground at Boo's window. There were four round impressions directly below it. I looked around the side of the house and found a step stool among some firewood. It had four round feet.

"There's my stool," Mrs. Heckler said. "I've been looking everywhere for that."

I opened it, and the legs fit neatly into the four holes. I moved the stool a few inches and stood on it.

"What are you doing?" she said.

"If I'm right, somebody got into your house using this." I stepped off. "I weigh a little less than 100 pounds."

"So?"

I moved the stool again and asked her to stand on it. She did and then got off, seeming perplexed.

I studied all three sets of holes. Hers were the deepest. "My weight left an impression, but not as deep as the first set. Yours are the deepest, so whoever got in here weighed a little more than me, but not as much as you."

She cocked one eyebrow. "You're not asking my weight, are you?"

I smiled. "I'll just guess. But it gives us something to go on."

We went back inside, and I got a pen and some paper and wrote:

> Aaron,
>
> I believe you. I don't think you did this, but you have to tell us the truth. What were you carrying home the night you met Ian? Talk to you soon.
>
> Bryce

CHAPTER 36

❀ Ashley ❀

"Why would someone frame him like that?" I said when Bryce told me about Boo's window.

"Could be somebody in high school. Maybe the trip to the lake will help."

I was getting ready for bed when Leigh came home. She dodged all of us and went straight to her room.

"Why is she crying?" Dylan said.

I knocked on her door, but there was no answer. I knocked louder.

"What?"

"I wanted to talk to you about Saturday."

"Give me a minute."

I went to Dylan's room to retuck him into bed. It was like walking through a Matchbox minefield. Everywhere you stepped, you hit something.

"Ashley, what does God look like?" Dylan said.

"Uh, well, God is a spirit, so he really doesn't look like you or me."

"But Jesus is God."

"Right." It was good to know he'd been paying attention in Sunday school.

"So if Jesus is God, what did *he* look like?"

I thought of all the flannel-board Jesuses I'd seen in my life—brown hair, beard, white face. "Well, we don't really know. Little kids ran to him, so he probably had a kind face. He was a carpenter, so he was strong and probably had rough hands. I've always kind of pictured him like Dad. . . ."

Dylan lay back on his pillow, his face scrunched up and concentrating on the car he held. "You mean Sam dad or our other dad?"

"Well, I guess he could look like either."

"Ashley?"

I love the way he says my name. It comes out in three syllables—Ash-uh-lee.

"How do you get a carpenter in your heart? Doesn't it hurt?"

I tried not to laugh, but I couldn't help it, and he looked like he was about to cry.

Before I could answer, Leigh called from her room, "Ashley? What did you want?"

"I'll be right back, okay?" I said to Dylan.

He nodded and yawned.

Leigh opened the door a sliver, and I told her what time we'd like to leave Saturday and where Bryce and I wanted to go. "You have anything planned with Randy?"

"No, that's fine." She closed the door.

I stood there a few moments, wondering if she might want to talk to somebody, but this was Leigh. The ice queen. The one with a shell as hard as a turtle's.

I wandered back down the hall to Dylan's room. The night-light made his face glow. His mouth was open, eyes closed, and he was breathing heavily.

"Good night, buddy," I whispered as I shut the door.

CHAPTER 37

Bryce

My cell phone beeped after class on Friday. Mom had left a message: "Bryce, Mrs. Heckler called and said she was heading home from Spring Hill. She asked if you'd meet her at her house after you get out of school. Love you!"

I caught up with Ashley, and she rode with me. We zigzagged through the gauntlet of middle schoolers and a line of cars.

There's a freedom about Fridays, a light-headed giddiness because you can stay up late and sleep in the next day. Eat popcorn and pizza, play video games until your thumbs are numb, watch movies.

It was chilly, and the leaves were long gone from the aspens. The Hecklers' driveway was as empty as the sky when we arrived. We knocked on the front door, but we both knew no one was there.

"One week from today," Ashley said.

"What?"

"Biggest shopping day of the year. Day after Thanksgiving."

"We should solve the money mystery so we can participate. You know, keep the economy moving."

She rolled her eyes. "We should solve it so you can buy me a nice birthday present."

Mrs. Heckler pulled up and parked. She had Jessie with her. "I'm sorry I'm late." She handed me a dirty envelope. "Aaron wanted me to give this to you. I haven't opened it."

I swallowed hard. Had I been wrong? Had Boo lied to us all along? I opened the envelope and pulled out a single sheet.

> Bryce,
>
> I didn't want to tell anybody about it, but since it looks like I'm going to be here awhile, you'd better show my mom. She can figure out what to do if it's still there.
>
> There's a rickety old barn near our house. Go to the loft and look in one corner. I kinda pushed hay around it.
>
> Thanks for helping me.
>
> Aaron

I led the way to the barn, and the others followed like I was the Pied Piper of Red Rock. A wooden ladder with mismatched steps led to the loft. I noticed a few bales of hay stacked in a square at one end. Then I heard a strange noise.

When I looked over the edge, it all came together.

"A kitty!" Jessie squealed as I held up the tiger-striped cat. It mewed and stretched. There were two empty cans of tuna inside the enclosure as well as a bowl of water.

"How sweet," Ashley said.

Mrs. Heckler frowned. "Why wouldn't he . . . ?"

"He's probably worried about his tough-guy image," Ashley said. "Bringing a stray kitten home and caring for it really ruins that kind of thing."

The woman smiled. "I never would have guessed."

"Me either," I said.

CHAPTER 38

Ashley

I was up early Saturday morning getting ready for the trip. Bryce had played video games till late, so I woke him up. His room smelled like the back room at our favorite pizza place, Big Mike's.

Leigh usually spends about four days putting on makeup and doing her hair, but she just pulled a baseball cap low and threw on some jeans and a sweatshirt.

"Why do they call it Devil's Paw, anyway?" Leigh said as we drove north on a two-lane road.

"Maybe they didn't want to call it Devil's Daddy," Bryce said.

I groaned. "It's paw, like foot, not father. It's the shape of the rock above the town—it kind of looks like a hoof. Plus a lot of mysterious things have happened to people there."

"Where'd you hear that, Marion Quidley?" Bryce said.

I didn't answer because that's exactly where I'd heard it. I changed the subject. "So, how's Randy?"

Leigh shrugged. "Who knows?"

"You two break up?"

She sighed. "You're supposed to be searching for the owner of that painting, not figuring out my love life. Where are we going first?"

"The library. Bryce will go to the post office, which is close."

"After that?" Leigh said.

I opened my memo pad. "A man who does estate sales."

We drove for about 20 minutes before we reached the turnoff to Devil's Paw. Leigh kept her iTunes blasting through the car speakers.

Pumpkins and cornstalks decorated driveways. You could almost smell Thanksgiving dinner cooking and hear the noisy reunions.

Leigh got turned around once and said a bad word, but we finally made it to the library just as it was opening. "I'll wait here," she said.

CHAPTER 39

Bryce

The library was a dinky little building with a gravel parking lot. I noticed the blue-and-white sign for the post office and took off.

Ashley had given me a couple of flyers with the picture on it. She included our home phone and my cell number. There were only a couple of people in line, so I waited my turn.

"You lose a dog or something?" the man said.

I explained the situation without telling him we'd found a treasure map and $37,400.

He looked at the flyer and shook his head. "Haven't seen that painting, but I'll ask our deliveryman. Tack it up right there.

"You might try the market just down the street," the man added. "They get a lot of traffic on the weekends. And the diner too."

CHAPTER 40

❀ Ashley ❀

The librarian was an older lady, white haired, glasses, nice smile. She had the demeanor of every librarian I've ever known—bright, interested, and ready to do anything she could to help.

She looked at the picture of the painting for a long time and then shook her head. "What's so special about this painting?"

"My brother and I found something inside it. We're looking for the owner."

She raised her eyebrows. "Isn't that something. Was it an old letter?"

"Sort of," I said, smiling.

"Did your parents make you do this?"

"No, it was our idea. My brother and me."

She cocked her head and smiled. "Well, tell you what I'm going to do. I'll put this in the bookcase at the front desk. Everyone will see it there."

I thanked her and went outside. Bryce returned and talked Leigh into walking downtown, so the three of us moseyed up the street. It was a quaint village with a souvenir shop/bookshop/general store, a tiny diner selling cider and donuts, and a market stocked with pumpkins, apples, and vegetables.

I walked into the diner and found a lady so busy that she made hummingbirds look lazy. She filled coffee mugs, yelled orders to the cook, and cleaned spills. When I asked if we could put something in the window, she said to come back Monday and talk to the manager.

The market had a bulletin board in the entry. There were lost dogs, found cats, and used cars. "Just put it up there," Leigh said.

We made one more stop, a coffee shop with old booths and tables that looked a hundred years old. The floor creaked when we walked inside, and a bell dinged. I don't care much for coffee—except Frappuccinos—but I love the smell.

Leigh ordered some Columbian but didn't offer to get us anything.

The man taking orders took my flyer and scanned it. "If you want to put it in the window, go ahead."

We walked slowly back to the library parking lot, hoping someone would run up and tell us they recognized the painting. No one did.

CHAPTER 41

Bryce

I had no idea what an estate sale was before all this happened. The two people we met, Mr. and Mrs. Landecker, looked like normal people with a normal house in the shadow of Devil's Paw. Before we showed them the picture, they opened their garage and explained a little about their business.

"We're usually hired by someone who's accumulated a lot of things or a person who's getting rid of their parents' belongings after they die," Mr. Landecker said.

"So you actually go to their house and set it up?" I said.

"Right. Or we sometimes take the belongings to auction."

Inside the garage were antique desks, chairs, dressers, old records, books, and lamps. These were leftovers from the last sale.

"Have you ever seen this picture?" Ashley said.

He took the paper and held it an arm's length from his face. "My wife usually handles the artwork," he said, handing the paper to her.

She held it out even farther. "If you're looking for something like this, the best place is an antique store in—"

"Actually, we're looking for the original owners," Ashley said. "We think they might live around here."

"Why do you think they'd live around here?"

"We found this inside the back of the painting," Ashley said, handing them the map.

"And you think this is Devil's Paw?" Mr. Landecker said. "This rock isn't right. It actually looks like Dynamite Peak."

"Yeah, I'd agree with that," his wife said. "This building right here looks like the old Peak mine."

"You mean we've been traipsing around this town for no reason?" Leigh said.

"Where is Dynamite Peak?" I said.

Mr. Landecker grabbed a map from his car. "About 10 miles as the crow flies. But the road to get there takes you maybe a half an hour."

"Ever do any estate sales over there?" Ashley said.

He shook his head. "Aren't many houses. Lots of people there who just want to get away."

CHAPTER 42

❀ Ashley ❀

There are many trails in an investigation, and you have to follow them until you find the right one. Bryce and I were happy to be going in the right direction, but Leigh was miffed.

"You never know," Bryce said. "Somebody from Devil's Paw could still get in touch with us."

"Thanks, Sherlock," Leigh said.

A green sign said Dynamite Peak, and we turned onto a smaller road that went straight up the mountain. The farther we went, the fewer houses we saw.

Leigh stopped for gas and complained about the price. Bryce grabbed a flyer and went inside the station.

I joined Leigh at the pump as numbers whizzed by. "What's wrong?"

She jerked her head around. "I don't like paying 25 cents more per gallon than at home."

I smiled.

"What?" she said.

"You sound like your dad."

That calmed her down a little and she looked away, smiling, I guess.

"You know, you can talk to me," I said. "I'm not going to blab anything."

"There's nothing to say."

"It's about Randy, isn't it?"

No response.

"He talked with Bryce and me. Asked our advice about you."

"When?"

"A while ago."

"What did he say?"

The conversation was vivid in my mind. Randy had said he'd been going to church, and things were starting to make sense to him. Though that was good, he said there was more and more distance between Leigh and him. Bryce and I had told Randy that we had been working on Leigh, praying for her for a long time.

"Well, he was kind of upset," I said, carefully choosing my words. "He's interested in church, but he doesn't want to lose you. He said he didn't think you'd like him if he became a religious wacko."

"He said that?"

I nodded. "He said he didn't want to wind up wearing Jesus stickers on his football jersey."

Leigh smiled and the pump clicked. She returned the handle and screwed the cap on. Then she folded her arms and leaned against her car. "He hasn't gone over to the dark side yet, but he's close."

Interesting that she thought becoming a Christian was going to the "dark side."

"You know, him going to church and stuff might actually make him a better boyfriend."

She scowled. "Maybe for you. He said he knows he'll have to give up a lot of stuff if he goes through with this. I would be one of them, and that's the way I'd want it." She closed the door to the gas tank.

"What are you afraid of? What's so scary about a guy seeing that there's more to life than football and baseball and getting drunk on the weekend? Randy wants more from life than that, and I think it's great."

"Is that what you think I want in life?" she said.

I hadn't chosen my words carefully enough.

"I know exactly what'll happen," Leigh said, her jaw tight. "He'll be just like you and your brother saying your prayers before bed and asking Dad to come to church. He'll pray for my soul and force me to listen to sermons on my iPod."

She turned and walked into the gas station.

CHAPTER 43

Bryce

Leigh looked like she had swallowed a gallon of gas when I passed her. "What's up with her?" I said to Ashley.

"Randy. She's worried he's turning into a TV preacher."

"He doesn't have the right hair for that job."

Ashley smiled, but I could tell it had been a tough conversation.

"This should cheer you up. I talked with the guy inside and showed him the painting."

"He recognize it?"

"No, but he let me put a flyer up, and he said there's a local paper that lists garage sales, estate sales, and stuff like that. They're open on Saturdays. Just up the road that way."

"Perfect!"

Leigh came back, and we piled into the car. I told her which direction to go, but she turned around.

"No, the newspaper place is the other—"

"I'm done. We're going home."

"What?" I said.

Ashley looked at Leigh like she wanted *us* to drink gasoline.

Leigh stopped and yelled, "I'm going home. I'm tired of chasing something we'll never find. We should keep the money and split it up instead of trying to be do-gooders."

Ashley reached for the door handle. "Let me out."

"Fine," Leigh said. She turned to me. "You want to stay too?"

"I-I . . ." It was hard to process what was happening. "Ash, get back in the car. We can call."

But Ashley had already jumped out and closed the door.

"Make up your mind, Sherlock," Leigh said.

I got out, closed the door, and watched Leigh speed away.

CHAPTER 44

✾ Ashley ✾

I was so mad I could spit bullets. I figured Leigh would turn around and get me, but gravel spun and she drove away.

"Guess Leigh's out of the money club, huh?" Bryce said, running up to me.

I growled like Pippin does when the FedEx guy comes to our house. "She's so closed-minded. She's going to throw Randy away because he's using his brain and thinking about God!"

"Calm down. I think she's upset with herself."

"How do you figure that?"

"She's backed into a corner. Her boyfriend is turning his back on her."

"But he's not—he's becoming the best person he can be."

"Sounds like you're interested in him. Ashley and Randy. Has a ring, doesn't it?"

"Stop."

"Sorry, I forgot you were waiting for Boo to get out of the slammer."

"That's not funny!"

I turned to her and held out my arms to ward off an attack. None came.

"I just don't want her to go through life mad at God and everybody else around her."

"I feel the same way, Ash, but Leigh doesn't want to date a disciple. She just wants a regular guy who'll score touchdowns, take her to the movies, and keep her company until she gets out of high school. Maybe that'll change, and maybe she'll get it, but for now that's the way it is."

"How are we going to get home?"

"She'll drive fast for about 10 miles with her music turned up. Then she'll slow down and not want to get caught by the police. Then she'll think of what Sam and Mom will say if she comes home without us—"

"Which won't be good."

"—and she'll turn around and burn more gas coming to get us."

"What if you're wrong?"

"We call Mom. In the meantime, keep walking."

I followed Bryce into the small town. We almost missed the newspaper office, it was so small. Bryce led the way, and a woman with thick glasses greeted us. The nameplate said Norma Welman, Editor and Publisher. The room smelled like cigarettes.

Bryce explained why we were here.

She looked at the photograph and shook her head. "Haven't seen that before. This looks old." She pointed to a stack of papers in the corner. "You can look through those for garage sales in the past year. Inside the back page."

Bryce and I sat in the corner, trying not to breathe the secondhand smoke. He'd find a garage sale in the paper, and I'd write down the phone number listed. We had gone all the way back to July when Bryce pulled out the map and showed it to Mrs. Welman. "Does this look familiar to you?"

She took off her glasses. "That's Dynamite Peak all right, but I don't recognize any of these landmarks. What are you kids looking for?"

I explained, and she asked what was inside the painting. "We'd rather not say, but we think it might be worth something."

She scratched her chin and looked at our handful of flyers. "I've got a proposition. My paper goes to the printer Monday, and I'm short a local story. Answer a few questions, and everyone in town will know about it."

CHAPTER 45

Bryce

Ashley and I answered Norma's questions, keeping the money and map a secret. She only used our first names in the article and asked people to call the newspaper office. Then she took an over-the-shoulder picture of us looking at one of our flyers. We were almost done when Leigh drove slowly past the newspaper parking lot.

Ashley saw her first and pointed. "Looks like you were right, little brother."

She likes to remind me that I'm less than a minute younger than her. We thanked Mrs. Welman and waved Leigh down.

The three of us sat—Ashley and me in the back—not saying a word. It felt weird being with Leigh and not hearing music blaring. She finally looked in the mirror and spoke as if nothing had happened. "Did you find out anything?"

"They're running a newspaper story about us next week," Ashley said.

We rode five miles before Leigh spoke again. "Have you talked with your mom?"

Fishing, I thought. *Time to play things cool.* "Been too busy to talk with anybody but the newspaper lady," I said.

Leigh nodded and her shoulders relaxed. "About what happened back there . . ."

"It's okay," Ashley said. "Really."

CHAPTER 46

❈ Ashley ❈

Saturday evening Mom took Bryce and me to shop for Thanksgiving dinner and our party. She took us to a discount grocery store, where you have to bag your own food. She was glad to hear that Ruth was coming, but she frowned when I told her the whole story.

Bryce and I bought separate chips and popcorn, pretzels and candy bars. The good stuff. We also bought frozen pizza, pizza bagels, mozzarella sticks, fried shrimp, barbecue chicken wings, and onion rings. There was no way we'd run out of food.

Bryce phoned Mrs. Heckler and talked a few minutes. He pursed his lips when he hung up. "Boo's anxious and seems scared. He thinks some kids are ganging up on him."

Mom turned. "What about the hearing?"

"The lawyer suggested he plead guilty. She says he'll get less time."

"But he's innocent," I said. "He shouldn't even be there." I felt bad that we had spent the whole day at Dynamite Peak.

"She said they may bring the case up this Wednesday." Bryce looked at Mom. "Do you think Ashley and I could follow up on something tomorrow morning?"

"And miss church?" she said.

Bryce nodded. "I hate to, but this is important."

Mom thought about it for a minute. "If this will help Aaron, I think you should go."

PART 6

THE LAKE

CHAPTER 47

Bryce

Ashley and I got up early, packed our stuff, and headed for the ATVs. It was chilly and we knew we wanted to ride fast, so we wore our heavy coats and riding gloves. The helmets cut a lot of the wind, but not all of it, and by the railroad tracks, my face was freezing.

The sun was up, and the rays of the orange ball lit patches of earth, like God was giving us directions. Scrub oak and aspens were bare. Pretty soon this whole area would be white with snow. I was glad for Boo's sake that there wasn't snow. No way we could look for clues in that.

Sam has explored a lot of the backcountry, so we asked him about the trail. He told us about a shortcut through a friend's farm. We cut through a field and found the trail, but we had to backtrack because a rockslide blocked our way. Finally we headed up the mountain.

It started out as a gentle slope but turned into a sharp incline. The trail became narrow, and Ashley let me go ahead. Suddenly the path dipped and curved. Before I knew it I was sliding downhill, my hand squeezing the brake, my tires searching for traction on the dew-covered ground. I almost bailed out, but I finally stopped three feet from a chasm, my heart pounding wildly.

Ashley pulled beside me and stepped off her machine to look over the edge. "You would have fallen a long time."

"I had it under control."

"Is that why you said all that in the microphone?"

We have headsets so we can talk to each other. "What did I say?"

"Nothing you'd want your Sunday-school teacher to hear."

I cringed. "Let's go."

CHAPTER 48

✻ Ashley ✻

I had known Bryce was going too fast, and I wished I'd have said something. When he neared the edge he said only one bad word and a lot of "Oh no, oh no!" type stuff. Looking back, it was kind of funny.

I looked down the ravine with its jagged rocks and trees. A tiny stream ran through it—quite a sight. But I was glad I wasn't looking at my brother's ATV.

The trail rose again and became tight with trees on either side. I noticed several No Trespassing and No Hunting signs in the distance.

Soon the path was overtaken by dead pine needles and disappeared. We found it again toward the top as it wound to our right around the mountain.

"Who do you think made this?" I said in the headset.

"Sam said they did it a long time ago when people were out of work. They built parks, dams, and roads. This project was probably done in the summer."

"Why?"

"Can you imagine them doing it with snow and howling winds?"

We came out on a ridge that opened up and gave us a view of the front range of mountains that stretches all the way from Colorado Springs past Denver. I could see why Boo spent time here. It was secluded and beautiful.

The path angled down again and overlooked a gently flowing stream. It moved toward a waterfall that worked its way through the gorge.

"Gorgeous," Bryce said, chuckling.

We finally made it to the lake—if you could call it that. We're from Illinois, where Lake Michigan makes any body of water in Colorado look like a mud puddle. We parked our ATVs behind some pine trees and headed for the rocky shore.

Bryce pulled out Boo's drawing and studied it. "I think he must have been over there when he saw the ATVs."

I grabbed a bag of chips out of my lunch stash and followed. We walked down an incline—slid is more like it—to the edge of the water. It lapped softly against the rocks.

Bryce picked at the rocks, looking at the trail, then back at Boo's drawing. "Here!" he yelled, kneeling on a rock.

A dead fish lay at his feet, and I suddenly didn't feel like eating the rest of my chips. Bryce studied it like it was a famous painting, but I couldn't stand the smell.

"Right here," Bryce said. "There's a little hole Boo must have made with his knife. He was telling the truth, Ash. This proves it."

CHAPTER 49

Bryce

I studied the footprints in the dried mud around the dead fish. Ashley and I don't do fingerprints or casts of shoes, but you have to look at everything available. I focused on one print with a weird, round shape. It had little ridges around the front, like a boot.

We poked around the area, searching for other clues, but didn't find any. I looked at my watch and realized the last morning worship service was about to begin at church. Funny how you think of things you care about when they're about to happen.

We walked the perimeter of the lake, skipping rocks (I beat Ashley with an eight-skipper) and finding old lures. Several fish surfaced looking for insects. Made me want to put a line in the water.

Ashley pointed out a discoloration in the water at the back of the lake. There was a white, frothy substance that looked like the foam on top of a root-beer float.

"What do you think that is?" Ashley said.

"Maybe it's mountain-lion pee."

"I'm serious."

"Probably just the runoff of the—"

"Bryce, look!"

The water was shallow, with a lot of silt and sediment. Several small fish floated on the surface.

"Reminds me of the time we watched the neighbor's fish for a week," I said.

Ashley didn't laugh. It was still a painful memory. "Why do you think they died?"

I shrugged. "Too young to die of old age."

I was getting hungry so I suggested we have our picnic. Ashley still seemed a little queasy, but she followed me to our ATVs.

The sun felt good on my face, and even though we were up higher, the temperature felt good. I had two ham sandwiches and some barbecue corn chips, along with three crunchy dill pickles.

Ashley got my attention and pointed at the back of the lake. A deer trotted down the hill and took a sip of water. The animal looked injured, its fur missing in places. Something spooked it, and the deer raised its head. With three jumps it was up the hill and out of sight.

CHAPTER 50

Ashley

Bryce stayed behind to finish his lunch, but I followed the deer to the ridge. I didn't have much of an appetite after seeing all the dead fish. Plus, there was something about the deer that bothered me. It moved fast but looked sick.

The deer was gone when I reached the top. Another stream ran through, probably runoff from the snowmelt above. The stream split off and part of it ran straight to the lake, but most gurgled and splashed toward the waterfall. It looked like the exact place Boo had described.

The breeze changed, and I noticed something in the air. A strong odor. I'm used to strong smells. We have two dogs who eat food that really stinks. I also clean out the barn at the alpaca farm, and I've been around horses and cows a lot, but this was different. Stronger.

I walked into the wind and found water with a slimy film on top pooled by the stream. It looked like the same froth we'd noticed at the lake.

Then I saw it. Down the incline lay a dead turtle, its head, legs, and body swollen. The smell was awful, and I called Bryce.

"Think *he* died of old age?" I said when he arrived.

"Could have been the flu." He moved closer and pushed it with a stick. I'm amazed at what my brother will do. "No signs of trauma," he said.

"Meaning?"

"He wasn't attacked by an animal. Looks like he was headed toward the lake and didn't make it."

"This is weird, Bryce. Why would fish and turtles be dying? This is the healthiest place on the planet."

Bryce shrugged. "You could take him back home and let the vet do an autopsy; otherwise I think it's time to go."

"What do you mean?"

Bryce looked at his watch. "There's still time to get home for the Broncos game."

"You've got to be kidding!"

A noise in the distance got our attention. It sounded like a chain saw at first, but as we moved toward the ridge we saw two ATVs coming straight up the trail toward us.

CHAPTER 51

Bryce

Ashley and I went into emergency mode, slipping behind some trees and heading toward our ATVs. We found a good spot in a clump of pine trees and watched. The two people rode giant ATVs. I'd seen them in catalogs but never this close. The tires were oversized, and the backs of both machines had been enlarged to carry barrels.

"What are they doing?" Ashley whispered.

"Maybe they're here to pick up the dead turtle."

They rode past the lake and up the ridge above us. As they passed, I noticed that both were wearing wading boots, the kind fly-fishermen use. They had on gloves as well.

"Are they going fishing?" Ashley said.

"Don't think so."

"We should get out of here."

I shook my head. "No, let's see what they do. Our ATVs are hidden well enough. When they're gone, we'll investigate."

They parked their machines on the ridge and loosened the straps holding the barrels. It took both of them to lift one barrel off the back and carry it out of sight.

"Wish we could see what's going on," Ashley said.

"Stay right here."

"Bryce, you're not going up there."

"I have to know what they're doing. I can follow these trees—"

"No." Ashley bit her lip. "What about that tree? I could climb up and see. Wouldn't be as risky."

I nodded.

CHAPTER 52

✾ Ashley ✾

I climbed with my helmet and gloves on. The second branch was hardest because it was higher and skinny, but I used the tree trunk to steady one leg and pulled myself up. As soon as I reached the third branch I could see the two people taking another barrel from their ATVs.

"See anything?" Bryce whispered in my headset.

"Yeah, but I can't see where they took the barrels. Is your cell phone off? I don't want it ringing."

"There's no service up here, but I just turned it off."

"Good." I reached for the limb above me and stood. "Okay, they're bent over by the stream. I'll go up one more limb."

"No. It's not worth the risk."

Something cracked beneath me.

"What was that?" said a deep-voiced guy at the stream.

I ducked and squatted.

"There! In the tree! Somebody's watching us!"

I've taken gymnastics for years, and my worst apparatus is the uneven parallel bars. I dived for the branch, and my feet plunged into the air.

CHAPTER 53

Bryce

I stood under the tree, waiting to catch Ashley, knowing I could only try to break her fall. Just as she was about to crash down on me, she grabbed the second branch, swung her legs past, and recovered.

I reached up and helped her down as the ATVs fired to life above us. We jumped on our ATVs and sped toward the trail. I raced ahead of Ashley and set the pace. *Concentrate on getting out of here, nothing else,* I said to myself.

"They're coming down the hill!" Ashley said in my headset.

"Don't look back," I said. "Just ride!"

We came over a ridge to a little clearing, and the trail flattened.

I kicked up speed, and Ashley stayed right on my tail. I warned Ashley about upcoming rocks. Then the trail turned sharply left and went straight downhill. I let the machine coast, keeping my hand off the accelerator, but as soon as I got to the bottom, I opened it up again and veered right.

"I think we're ahead of them," I gasped. "Keep going or hide?"

"Where? There's nothing but pine trees."

She was right. No matter where we went, we'd be exposed. I gunned the engine and shot up a little incline; then it was straight down again.

"Think they know a shortcut?" Ashley said.

It made me wonder, but after riding the trail, I couldn't imagine a shortcut from the lake. "Keep going," I said.

CHAPTER 54

❈ Ashley ❈

I glanced back quickly but didn't see the ATVs. I told Bryce that the two people had either given up or had taken some other path.

A few minutes later Bryce slid to a stop in the middle of a clearing. I bumped the rear end of his ATV, and we turned off our machines. Nothing but the wind blowing through the trees.

"You think they gave up on us?" I said.

Bryce shrugged and turned on his cell phone, but he still had no signal. "Let's keep going and be careful to—"

A noise from behind startled me, and Bryce stared. I turned just as one of the ATVs flew over the ridge, all four wheels lifting off the ground. It looked like a professional driver in one of those car commercials.

"Hit it!" Bryce said.

He started his ATV and rushed away, but mine sputtered and coughed. I knew it had enough gas, so I tried again. This time it came to life. I've never gunned the engine before, and I thought the thing was going to pop a wheelie and throw me to the ground. I regained control and followed Bryce down the hill.

Suddenly, from the edge of the tree line, the other ATV appeared and headed right for us. "Bryce, watch out!"

Bryce kept going, straight for the other guy. It was the game of chicken we used to play with our bikes. The driver stopped and jumped off, blocking us, but Bryce is an expert at maneuvering his ATV. He jumped off the path, over a couple of rocks, and narrowly missed a tree.

I followed a little slower, but I made it as the other driver zoomed up.

CHAPTER 55

Bryce

The guy on the ATV was wearing a dark helmet and visor, so I couldn't tell anything about him other than he was big. I was proud of Ashley. She followed close as the trees whizzed by, the toughest part of the trip.

I glanced back and saw one ATV following us. Part of me was scared that these two would hurt us. The other part was excited we had stumbled onto more clues. This would have to help Boo.

My head was turned, looking at the ATV trailing us, when Ashley yelled, "Brake! Brake!"

The hairpin turn was just ahead, the one I'd almost gone over earlier. I slammed on my brakes and skidded in the moist earth.

CHAPTER 56

✽ Ashley ✽

I wanted to close my eyes, but I couldn't. My brother was sliding toward certain death as he neared the drop-off. The back end of his ATV slid to the right, toward a huge pine tree, then slid left. He was slowing, but would he stop in time?

"Jump!" I shouted.

I knew if he did that the ATV would be lost, smashed against the rocks, but better that than a smashed brother. You can buy another ATV. You can't buy a brother like Bryce. (Although I've told him that Mom and Dad really bought him at Kmart.)

I held my breath as Bryce stayed with the ATV. It finally came to rest at the ledge. A small tree had stopped him from going over.

Before I could say anything, the other ATV shot past me and headed straight for my brother. "Bryce, watch out!"

Bryce saw him coming and gunned his engine, spinning his tires and speeding away.

The other driver didn't have time to correct—his ATV careened toward the drop-off. The driver jumped just before his ATV hurtled over the edge. He hit the pine needles with a thud and rolled a few yards.

I looked over the edge and saw the ATV crash into a huge rock, then twist and slam into a tree. In movies the thing would have burst into flames and exploded, but this was real life.

"Ashley, come on!" Bryce said.

"What about him? What if he's hurt?"

"He just tried to push me off that cliff!"

I slowed as I passed the driver, looking for any movement. Suddenly an arm moved, and the guy jumped up and raced toward me.

I stomped on the gas and spun a mix of pinecones, rocks, and mud into his face.

He shook his fist at us as we drove out of sight.

CHAPTER 57

Bryce

Ashley and I finally made it back to the train tracks, covered in mud and glad to be near civilization. The streets of Red Rock looked deserted, and I figured it was because of the Broncos game.

We parked our ATVs at Mrs. Watson's house and walked to the police station. The front door was locked, so I called the emergency number and got the patrolman on duty. I explained that we had just been attacked and described the two drivers. I also told him that one ATV was at the bottom of the gulch, probably smashed into a billion pieces.

"What were you doing back there?" the officer said.

I told him a friend of ours had been accused of a crime, and we had evidence that would clear him.

The officer didn't seem convinced. "We're short staffed today," he said. "I'll log the call, and you can come in tomorrow and give a full report."

"But they'll be gone by tomorrow!" I said.

"Best I can do for you, kid," the officer said.

I hung up, wishing I could slam it down, but you can't do that with a cell phone. Then I got an idea. "Come on, Ash!"

Adrenaline pumped as I found Ian's house. The front door was open, and I could hear the Broncos game loud through the screen door. Someone yelled and whooped as a Broncos wide receiver caught a pass for a first down.

I knocked on the door, thinking Ian's mom or dad would come.

Instead, it was Ian himself. "Hey, Timberline—why aren't you home watching the game?" He looked at Ashley and smiled. "Hi there."

There was no way he could have made it home from the trail this fast; plus it looked like he had just gotten out of bed.

"Yeah, I forgot about it," I said. I turned and we walked away.

PART 7

QUESTIONS

CHAPTER 58

⌘ Ashley ⌘

Thanksgiving week is exciting because our birthday is close, it's a short school week, and there's special food in the cafeteria.

For Bryce and me, however, that Monday was awful. We kept glancing over our shoulders, expecting ATV riders to come looking for us.

In Spanish class Mrs. Sanchez asked why Boo wasn't in class. I guess she hadn't checked her e-mail. One kid said he had been sentenced to two years at Spring Hill. "We'll probably never see him again."

"Good riddance," another kid said.

It took everything in me to keep quiet.

Mrs. Sanchez seemed troubled by the reports, and after everyone left, I went up to her. “I just wanted you to know that there’s a chance Fernando may be back at school.” She’d had us take Spanish names on the first day, and that’s the one Boo had chosen.

“Really?” she said.

I told her that Bryce and I had gone with Mr. Forster to see him and that he might be innocent.

Her face brightened, and she put a hand on my shoulder. “I’m glad to see you’re being a friend to someone who doesn’t have many.”

At lunch, Hayley and Marion were as excited as I’d ever seen them. They couldn’t stop talking about the party Wednesday, and Hayley said she’d already bought my present.

When she left, Marion wouldn’t make eye contact.

“What’s wrong?” I said.

She put down a stalk of asparagus. “It’s about your present. I’m not sure . . .”

I knew Marion’s family struggled with money because her dad was sick. It was all her mom could do to keep the house running.

“Marion, I didn’t invite you for the present you could bring. I want you there because I know it’ll be a lot more fun.”

“What do you want?” she said.

I knew I couldn’t say nothing, because everyone was going to bring a present. “A gift certificate to a bookstore or Starbucks would be great.”

Marion’s whole body seemed to relax. “Hey, maybe I could get you both!”

CHAPTER 59

Bryce

After school Ashley and I went straight to the police station to file our report. Officer Ormsby was surprised to see us and hadn't heard about our call. He shuffled through papers and went into another room. He came back reading our report from a call log.

Ashley looked upset, and I tried to calm her. "They're gonna help."

"But how long will it take?" she said. "If they haven't gone back there, we're looking at tomorrow before we can show the evidence to Boo's lawyer."

"If his lawyer will even look at it."

We told our story to Officer Ormsby, and he took notes. When we told him the part about the guy on the ATV trying to run Bryce off the cliff, he stared at us. "Did you report that yesterday?"

I nodded. "The officer I talked with acted kind of suspicious as he talked to me. I don't think he believed us."

He pulled out another sheet from the stack. "There was another call that came in just before yours. It was about two kids on ATVs joyriding on private property."

I looked at Ashley. "We're definitely on to something." I turned to the officer. "Do you know who made the phone call?"

He frowned. "It's listed as anonymous, and the phone ID said *unavailable.*"

"When will you go up there to investigate?"

"This evening."

CHAPTER 60

❋ Ashley ❋

After the police station, Bryce and I rode our bikes to Mile High Disposal. Bryce wanted to talk with Ian Connor again, and I tagged along.

The dump was a plot of land on the outskirts of town. A row of big timbers served as a gate, and barbed wire circled the property. Weeds grew around old cars parked inside the fence. Mounds of plastic trash bags were piled in a ravine behind the main building. It wasn't the most pleasant-smelling place I'd ever been.

Ivy grew near a barnlike structure, and a black dog with jaws the size of a snowblower was chained near the entrance. He gave a low growl, all the warning we needed.

"Can I help you?" a heavyset man said. He had wide sideburns and jet-black hair—too dark for his age—and threw a couple of tires behind a smashed car.

"So this is where they bring all the wrecks," I said.

"You talking about me or the cars?" he said. Then he threw back his head and laughed. "We call these slightly dented."

"Are you Ian's uncle?" Bryce said.

"Sure am. You know him?"

"I met him the other day. Is he around?"

"No, out on an errand. Should be back soon. You looking for something?"

"ATV parts," Bryce said.

He pointed. "All the ATVs are back there. Take a look."

We walked through a sea of old tires, refrigerators, washing machines, dishwashers, and cars. Fire had gutted two huge RVs parked along the fence. Bikes, motorcycles, lawn mowers, and farm equipment were jammed into the yard.

We turned a corner and stared at an ATV convention—only it wasn't a convention you'd want to visit. Wheels had been stripped off, frames were cracked, handlebars bent into impossible positions. People had scavenged bits and pieces from each machine—a gas tank here, a speedometer there.

Bryce had turned to leave when I spotted something. "Look at that."

Behind the rest of the ATVs and covered with a tarp was the back of a wrecked machine. Bryce and I climbed over the others, hopping from seat to seat. We pulled the tarp off and found a severely mangled ATV. The straps on the back platform were gone, but I knew where I'd seen it.

"Bryce, this is the ATV that tried to run you into the ravine."

"See something?" Ian's uncle said.

"Yeah, this one," Bryce said. "Do you know when it was brought in?"

The man chuckled. "Had to have been some time ago because we always put the newer stuff in front."

"Do you remember who brought it?" I said.

The man shook his head. "Sometimes people bring stuff in I don't even see. Ian's here during the day while I'm out." He narrowed his eyes. "What do you want with that particular machine?"

"We saw this one yesterday," Ashley said.

"Yesterday? You were out here looking through the yard?"

"No, we—"

"Because the neighbors complained this morning. Said there was something going on up here late last night. Noises. A truck or two. Know anything about it?"

"Come on, Ash," Bryce whispered.

"We weren't here," I said. "And maybe we're mistaken. It probably is just some old clunker."

We left the junkyard with more questions than answers.

CHAPTER 61

Bryce

Since Officer Ormsby didn't call, I phoned him after nine that night and was told he was still on patrol.

The phone rang a few minutes later. It was the noisiest phone call in history, with people yelling and laughing in the background. "Hello?" I said.

"Bryce?" A weak voice. Soft and scared.

"Yeah, who's this?"

"Aaron."

Boo. "What's up?"

"My mom wasn't home, so I called you."

"How are you?"

"A lot better after I got your note. I didn't think there'd be anyone who believed me. I don't even think my mom believes me."

"She loves you a lot."

"Yeah, I guess."

"Any news on the hearing?"

His voice got softer. "They're saying it's going to happen Wednesday."

"No."

"Have you found out anything?"

I told him about our trip to the lake. I didn't go into detail about the ATV chase, but I said we'd found evidence at the dump. "Is there a chance Ian's uncle would have something against you?"

"I don't even know the guy."

"Would Ian have set you up?"

"I swear, Bryce, the only reason I talked to him was to get that car part."

"How did you get in touch with him?"

Boo thought for a moment. "He called me. Said someone had told him I was working on an old car and asked if I needed a part."

"Wait—Ian called you out of the blue?"

"Yeah."

"Did he say who told him you were working on a car?"

He paused, and I heard someone talk over the loudspeaker. Things got really quiet. "I don't think he did, but I can't remember. . . ."

The phone muffled, and it sounded like Boo put a hand over the receiver. "Stop it!" he said.

Someone cursed. "You fooled around and messed it up for us. Now we don't get to use the phone until tomorrow!"

I heard a smack, then a tussle, and the phone crashed against something. More bad words. Then someone whistled, and people started clapping and yelling.

"Get him!" a guy hollered.

"Harder!" someone else said.

"Yeah, we got a fight now!"

It was torture listening to the bad language and yelling. Finally the noise stopped, and a man with a deep voice told them to break it up. Someone hung up the phone, and it was like cutting a lifeline to a person lost at sea.

The phone rang again. It was Officer Ormsby. "I made it back there before dusk and had a look around."

"Let me guess," I said. "You didn't see any ATV at the bottom of the ravine."

"Right. And above the lake there was nothing you mentioned—no ATV tracks, drums, or dead turtles. Just clear, pristine mountain country."

Someone got to it before he went there, I thought. "Thanks for looking, Officer. We really appreciate it."

CHAPTER 62

⌘ Ashley ⌘

Bryce told me about Boo and what Officer Ormsby had said. I closed my eyes and imagined Boo being pummeled by some bully.

As Bryce dialed Mrs. Heckler, he looked at me. "You need to get a prayer request out to as many as you can. We only have one day unless the hearing gets postponed."

I logged on to our church Web site and the e-mail prayer chain. We don't go to a megachurch, but there are more than 200 people on the list. The other requests were mostly about surgeries and sicknesses. I tried to write as grown-up as I could.

> Please pray for a Red Rock middle schooler who has been falsely accused of a crime. Pray that he will remain safe in the juvenile detention center, that his hearing will be postponed, and that new evidence concerning his innocence will be allowed.

I read over the note and made a few changes. Then I added:

> And please pray that this experience will cause him to consider a relationship with God.

CHAPTER 63

Bryce

The next day Ashley and I met at lunch and compared notes. We both thought Ian knew more than he was telling.

"We never looked for a serial number or a sticker from the store that sold the ATV," I said. "I say we go back to the dump and look at it one more time."

Ashley agreed and picked at her sandwich. "Know what I'd do with the money in the painting if it were ours?" she whispered. "Hire a good lawyer for Boo."

I could think of better things than a lawyer to spend the money on, but I nodded.

Marion walked up and smiled at me. To think of her at our house all night gave me the willies, but she had become a good friend to Ashley. She didn't seem quite as kooky as when we first met her.

After school Ashley and I rode our bikes to the dump and hid them in some bushes. Ian's car was parked outside the gate. We moved closer, cutting through some scrub oak. There were signs up to watch out for bears in the area, tanking up for their winter hibernation.

A pickup loaded with scraps of wood and metal passed. Ian's uncle came out and talked with the driver. Ian walked over and helped unload the man's junk.

Ashley and I moved to the side and found the tarp from the day before. I found a long stick, shoved it through the chain-link fence, and moved it. The ATV was gone.

Ashley pointed. "Look over there."

The ATV sat in front of a big contraption. It wasn't until the pickup left and Ian pushed the ATV inside with a tractor that I figured out what it was. By then it was too late.

Ian hit a switch, and two walls pushed together, like the garbage-disposal scene in *Star Wars*. When the ATV was crushed sideways, a huge piece of metal smashed it from above. The whole thing wound up the size of a wastebasket.

Ashley looked at me. "Guess we'll never find the serial number on that hunk of junk. What now?"

Ian's uncle gestured at a stack of pallets and returned to his office. He emerged a few minutes later with his jacket and a lunch box. He waved at Ian, got in his truck, and pulled away.

"Maybe if you talked with Ian's mother, she could help," I said.

"And what will you do?"

"Stay here until Ian's done."

Ashley squinted at me. "Don't do anything stupid."

CHAPTER 64

❀ Ashley ❀

I pecked on Mrs. Connor's front door, but there was no answer. I knocked a little harder, and she finally came to the door in her bathrobe.

"Can you talk a minute?" I said, my voice pleading, trying to make my face look as angelic as I could. "It's about Ian."

"Did he do something to you?" she said, her face clouded in fear.

I thought it was a strange question. "No, but someone might get hurt unless he helps my brother and me."

She opened the door. "Come inside."

It was an older house with lime green walls and gold door handles that looked 50 years old. The carpet was worn down to the padding, and the kitchen tile had cracks in it.

Mrs. Connor offered me something to drink, but judging from all the newspapers, unopened mail, and clutter on the table, I figured there was no way she could fit a glass there.

"I have some grape juice if you'd like it," she added.

I love grape juice and said I'd take it.

She opened the cupboard, and there was only one mug left. The rest of the glasses and cups were piled high in the sink. She handed me a full glass. "You look a little young to be friends with Ian."

"Actually, I don't know him well. But there was a question I thought you could answer."

"What's that?"

"Other than his uncle, does Ian have any other employer?"

She furrowed her eyebrows. "I need to know what this is about."

She looked like a compassionate woman, one who had probably had her share of trouble. I told her about Boo and what he'd been through the past few years.

"And what does this have to do with Ian?"

I told her that Ian had met him the same night of the break-in at Red Rock Crossing, and she seemed startled.

"Do you know something that might help our friend?"

CHAPTER 65

Bryce

Ian locked the front gate and ambled toward his car. He seemed to have no idea I'd been watching him or that I had crawled into his backseat.

He got in and started the car. When I sat up I thought he was going to jump out of his skin. "What are you doing in here?"

"Need to talk," I said.

He slammed the car into park and yelled at me to get out.

"How did you know Aaron needed a car part?" I said.

His eyes flashed.

I didn't give him the chance to yell again. "The police will know that ATV is here. The one you crushed. My sister and I saw the whole thing."

"I don't know what you're talking about."

"Sure you do. You met somebody up here Sunday night and let them in so they could junk the machine. Then they told you to destroy the evidence."

He shook his head. "You're in way over your head, kid. Leave this alone and go back to your playground."

"A friend of ours is in trouble. He doesn't deserve it, and you can clear this up."

"Heckler is just getting what's coming to him," Ian said.

"For something he didn't do?"

"I'm telling you, stay out of this. You and your sister—"

"We saw what they were doing at the lake." The strength in my voice surprised me because inside I was shaking. "Tell me who it is, and we'll leave you alone."

Ian gritted his teeth. "Listen. This is not a game. These people are playing for keeps, and they won't have any trouble making sure they keep you quiet."

"How are you involved?"

He got out of the car and opened my door. "Get out."

"Ian, they're using you. What do you get out of this?"

He grabbed me by the shirt and pulled till it ripped at the collar. "Leave me alone. Understand? I see you out here again and I'll tell them about you."

CHAPTER 66

⌘ Ashley ⌘

Mrs. Connor wiped tears away as she told me what she suspected. "Ian's always spent the money as fast as he's paid. Then one day he came home with that car. I couldn't understand it and asked him how he got the money."

"What did he say?"

"A friend had given him a loan and that I shouldn't worry."

I tried to lay out the pieces of the puzzle in my mind, but they weren't coming together. "Do you have any idea who?"

"Ian is almost 20, and I don't see that much of him."

I understood. When Leigh got her own car it was like a stranger moved into our house. She was house-sitting or at a part-time job or doing stuff at school all the time.

"This boy that you said is in trouble—what's his name?"

I told her and filled in the missing pieces of his story. "Now his mom and dad are having a hard time. I think they've separated."

"And you say he was sent to the juvenile detention center?"

I nodded.

"Why would Ian want someone to be punished for something he didn't do?"

"We think Aaron might have seen something he shouldn't have. The people he saw had him put away." I leaned closer to Mrs. Connor. "They're having the hearing for Aaron—maybe tomorrow. If we can bring evidence that he's innocent, it could really help."

"Write your number down on this," she said, picking up a notepad from the pile on the table. "I'll talk with Ian tonight."

CHAPTER 67

Bryce

It was a quiet dinner, the kind where you hear silverware clink. Mom made ramen noodles and cheese chips and salsa—I guess she was getting our stomachs ready for the party and Thanksgiving.

"So the big story comes out in the paper tomorrow, huh?" Leigh said to Ashley. "If nobody calls, how long will you wait before you spend the money?"

"Somebody will call," Ashley said. "I'm sure of it."

Leigh wiped her mouth with a napkin. "Well, I need money for the gas we wasted."

I couldn't believe my ears. "Hey, you agreed to help us if you got a percentage. You're taking the same risk—"

Leigh slammed her spoon into her noodles, splashing Dylan. "I didn't know you'd make such stupid decisions—"

"Leigh," Sam interrupted.

Dylan cried and wiped his shirt. "She got me all ramen noodly!"

Sam pulled $20 out of his wallet and handed it to Leigh. "Here."

Leigh snatched the money.

Dylan cried his way to the laundry room, looking for a dry shirt.

"This means you're out of the loop with their find," Sam said to Leigh.

"Fine. I don't want their stupid money." She raced upstairs.

The phone rang, interrupting our noodle slurping. After what Ashley had told me about meeting Mrs. Connor, I figured it would be for her.

Instead, Mom handed it to me. "It's Mrs. Heckler."

"I'm glad you called," I said. "We have a new development. Ashley and I have—"

"Bryce?"

I was so excited that I kept on going. "If you haven't talked with Aaron, you have to let him know what we found out."

"Bryce? I have news."

"Is Aaron coming home for Thanksgiving?"

"No." Her voice was flat. "Bryce, I want you to know how much I appreciate all you've done. . . ."

"Mrs. Heckler, we're waiting on a call right now that could break this whole thing wide-open."

"Yes. Well, there isn't going to be any need to do that. Aaron has confessed."

"What?"

"He spoke with a counselor and told him the truth. The hearing is a formality now. They've moved that to Monday."

"And what happens to him?"

"Part of the deal is that he'll be moved to one of the other pods," she said, her voice cracking. "If he doesn't get into any more trouble, he'll get out in two years."

"Two years? Mrs. Heckler, this is not right. You know he didn't break into that drycleaners!"

Ashley came up behind me, a concerned look on her face.

"Like I said, I'm grateful for all you and your sister have done."

"But if we have evidence that proves—"

"Bryce, he confessed," Mrs. Heckler said, breaking down.

I felt awful. I hate hearing people cry, especially mothers. It was such a mournful thing that I could hardly stand it. I wanted to tell her that Aaron had confessed because he'd been attacked. He'd probably do anything to get out of his pod. But the more she cried, the longer I kept quiet.

She tried to thank me again and then hung up.

"What was that about?" Ashley said.

I told her.

"This is not over," she said.

"Ashley, he confessed."

The phone rang and Ashley grabbed it. When she hung up, her face told the story. "Mrs. Connor said Ian doesn't know anything about the lake or what happened to Boo. If we come to her house again, she said she'll call the police."

I sat down hard on the couch. Something was wrong with our church's prayer chain.

PART 8

THE PARTY

CHAPTER 68

❀ Ashley ❀

The next day I didn't feel like having a birthday party, but we couldn't cancel it. Mom brought a copy of the Dynamite Peak newspaper during lunch. Bryce and I were the cover story—our picture was on the front, our backs to the camera. The headline read "Children Looking for Painting's Owner."

I didn't much care for the word *children,* but the article was surprisingly good. Mrs. Welman had written it in a mystery style but never revealed what we had found.

"Wonder if she's gotten any calls," Bryce said.

When we got home from school, Mom put in a DVD of us right after we were born. Bryce was pink and wiggly, and our skin looked like dried prunes. Our dad had taken the video and seemed happy. I looked at Sam a couple of times during the video. I don't know if he feels threatened by our love for our real dad, but if he does, he doesn't show it.

Dylan squealed at the babies on-screen and had a hard time understanding it was us. The doorbell rang, and I looked at my watch. Too early for any of our guests.

I opened the door and saw Randy, Leigh's boyfriend. Leigh came out of her room and stood at the top of the stairs. Randy smiled at her and shook Sam's hand, then pulled out two wrapped packages from behind his back.

"You didn't have to do this," I said.

"I wanted to," he said.

I opened mine and found a really pretty hardback diary.

"I got it from Juicy Pages. Mr. Forster picked it out. You can return it for something else if you don't like it."

"I love it!" I said, and I hugged him.

Bryce opened his and pulled out a hooded sweatshirt from the high school. "I've been wanting one of these!"

There was an awkward silence as Randy shoved his hands in his pockets. "Well, I guess I'd better be going."

"You want to stay for pizza?" Mom said. "There's going to be plenty."

He glanced up at Leigh. "I'd like to, but I think I'd better get home." He nodded at Leigh, then looked at us. "Happy birthday, you guys."

CHAPTER 69

Bryce

One by one the guests arrived with their sleeping bags, pillows, and presents. Marion Quidley wanted Ashley to open her card as soon as she got there. The card had the Loch Ness monster on the front and a funny birthday greeting. Inside the card were a couple of gift certificates, which I don't care for, but Ashley seemed excited.

When Duncan Swift arrived, Ashley moved to the back of the room and kept quiet. Duncan and I joked and kicked a Hacky Sack around with Kael and Chuck until the pizza was ready.

The one squirrelly thing happened with Ruth's mom. She went over her rules with Mom about TV shows and movies and stayed a long time.

The guys finally grabbed our pizzas and headed to the barn. In the loft beside Sam's office is another room where we play video games and Sam has some exercise equipment. He had moved the big TV from downstairs into that room and had stored the exercise equipment so we wouldn't be cramped.

We set up our four controllers and played a new NFL game. When we got bored, we switched to an ATV game. We ate pizza, drank soda (Dr Pepper is my favorite), and talked about girls, movies, the Broncos, and school.

It should have been the best night of my life, but all I could think about was Boo. I wondered what he would do for Thanksgiving and if they served turkey in the detention center. I also thought about Ian. Were Ashley and I in over our heads?

"Come on, Timberline. What's your problem?" Duncan said after my ATV went over a cliff. "You gotta concentrate!"

CHAPTER 70

⌘ Ashley ⌘

The family room was reserved for the girls, and I pulled out some board games. It was fun to see how good Marion was, figuring out strategies and trying to win. If you don't think females are competitive, you should come to one of my birthday parties.

Someone mentioned Boo, and Marion said she'd heard a rumor. "It's nothing new, just that Boo pled guilty and is being sent to the adult prison."

The phone rang upstairs, and Mom said it was for me.

The girls giggled and mentioned Duncan's name. "Bet he asks you to meet him for a moonlight stroll," Hayley said.

I rolled my eyes and took the phone.

It was Mrs. Welman, and she sounded excited. "Did you see a copy of the paper today?"

I told her we had and that it was a good article.

"I just got a call—I don't know why I didn't think of this before."

"Think of what?"

"The Willoby estate. It's at the edge of the mountain on about 100 acres. Big old house. Lots of trees."

"What about it?"

"The husband and wife died last spring. A car accident."

I vaguely remembered something about a couple who had gotten mixed up in some construction and had gone the wrong way on the interstate.

"A friend of theirs phoned me," Mrs. Welman continued. "She remembered seeing that picture hanging upstairs, just outside the daughter's room."

"Daughter?"

"Yes, the Willobys had a child. A daughter who ran off. They patched things up, but the story is, things were never the same. The daughter was trustee of the property, and what she didn't sell, she carted off to charity."

"Which is how we got the painting."

"Looks that way. Only the story gets a little sad."

"What could be sadder?"

"The friend who called said the daughter had loads of money after the sale, but she spent a lot on trips. She put some into an investment scheme, and basically she lost the whole thing."

"That's awful."

"Yeah, and from what the lady told me, the mother and father were fine people, churchgoers. She said they prayed day and night for that girl."

"Do you know where the daughter lives? her name?"

"Selena Willoby. Last the friend heard she moved to Las Vegas."

CHAPTER 71

Bryce

I sat by the computer in the living room as Ashley typed in the woman's name. Sam had come to the barn to get me. The other guys finished the video game without me.

"What's this about?" Marion said. "Why are you guys so excited?"

Mom handed Marion the newspaper article, and she read it faster than Chuck can gobble pizza, which is like lightning. "This is you guys? Why didn't I hear anything about this?"

A smile crept up the corner of Ashley's mouth. "I got something."

A Selena Willoby was listed as a resident of Las Vegas, with an address on Sandhill Court. Ashley wrote the number on a scrap of paper, her hands shaking.

"Las Vegas is an hour behind us, so the time's not a problem," Marion said.

Ashley handed me the phone.

"Why me?"

"I found her. You call."

I dialed the number cautiously, trying to figure out what I was going to say. *Hello, Selena, we found $37,400 in an old picture and think it belongs to you* didn't seem like a good approach.

Beep, beep, beep. "The number you have dialed is not correct or is not in service at this time," a woman's voice said. "Please check the number and dial again."

I hit the Speakerphone button and let everyone hear. "Looks like Selena is not in Vegas," I said.

Marion sat and opened a different Web site. She typed in *Selena Willoby* and did a whole-state search. Nothing came up. Then she typed in *Utah,* which is right next to Nevada. Again, nothing.

"You could type in all 50 states and still not find her," Hayley said.

"Should we start with Alabama?" Marion said.

"You're never going to find her," Ruth said.

"Do the western states," I said.

Marion smiled and typed in *Oregon, Washington,* and *California* and moved her way east. It wasn't until she got to Colorado that she hit pay dirt.

"Bingo. *Selena Willoby. Woodland Park.*"

"That's not far," Ashley said. "Isn't that about an hour from here?"

I nodded, wrote the number down, then handed Ashley the phone. "We did the work. You call."

CHAPTER 72

❀ Ashley ❀

I was getting a dose of my own medicine, but I didn't care. I wanted to talk with Selena Willoby. I took the phone into my room so I could concentrate.

"Hello?" a man said.

"Hi, I'm looking for Selena."

"Not here. Who's this?"

"My name is Ashley. I'm—"

"If you're selling something, I'm not interested."

For a second I thought about hanging up. "I'm not selling anything. I'm trying to get something back to Selena."

"What?"

"A painting. We found something inside it."

Silence.

Instead of waiting for another question, I fired one of my own. "How long has Selena lived there?"

"We moved in a couple of months ago."

"From Las Vegas?"

"Yeah." He sounded wary, like he expected the FBI to raid him at any minute. "What was in the painting?"

"I'd rather not say over the phone. Do you know when Selena will be back?"

"She's at work down at the Quick Mart. Won't be home till tomorrow morning."

Working all night on Thanksgiving Eve. At a gas station. Didn't sound like she had much of her parents' money left. "The one in Woodland Park?"

"Yeah. If you give me your number—"

I hung up and ran into the hall. Sam was coming out of the bathroom. "Could you drive us to Woodland Park tonight?"

CHAPTER 73

Bryce

I could understand Ashley's excitement, but there wasn't enough room in Sam's truck for all of us to go. Sam said if it was what Ashley wanted to do on her birthday, he would take her.

The only problem was Ruth. She said her parents wouldn't like an unscheduled trip. Ashley, Hayley, and Marion tried to convince her it would be fun, but she called her mom to pick her up.

We all ate birthday cake while the girls waited for Ruth's mother. My stomach was so full of pizza I could hardly move. Mom took pictures, and Dylan danced around the living room in his Batman costume—with his Spider-Man underwear showing in the back.

As soon as Ruth left, Ashley grabbed the painting and headed for Sam's truck. She promised she'd call when they found Selena. Dylan cried about going with them, and Mom grabbed him, except she ripped off one of his bat ears, and he screamed like it was *real.*

Two minutes after they were gone, the phone rang. It was Ruth. "Mom thought I should tell you. When we pulled out of your driveway, our headlights flashed on someone behind your barn. He was walking around back there."

"You trying to scare me?" I said playfully.

"No. I swear."

I thanked her and asked the guys if any of them had been out there. When they said they hadn't, I grabbed one of our big flashlights, the 10-pounder.

"Let's get 'em!" Duncan said.

We ran out, the guys whooping and hollering, which was kind of dumb. We looked around the barn and in the field but didn't find anyone.

"Probably just her imagination," Kael said.

CHAPTER 74

⌘ Ashley ⌘

Sam kept the radio low as we drove the curvy road to Woodland Park. I thought I was going to toss my pizza, so I rolled my window down a little and everyone complained.

Marion asked why Ruth couldn't go, and I tried to explain.

Marion pulled a piece of paper out of her pocket. "She gave me this before she left."

A tract. It explained about God and Jesus and how to become a Christian. It made me mad—not that I think tracts are bad, but giving it at my birthday party frosted me.

"She gave me one too," Hayley said, holding out the same tract.

Marion took hers back from me.

"I'm sorry," I said. "Ruth is . . . well . . . enthusiastic."

Sam looked at me out of the corner of his eye, but I just stared straight ahead.

"What's the plan?" Marion said as we got closer. "You going in and telling her about the money?"

"No, I want to see if she recognizes the painting."

"I don't get it," Hayley said. "That money is yours."

I tried to explain, but Hayley and Marion looked at me like I had an extra eye in my forehead.

"If you didn't feel right about keeping it, you could have given it to the school sign fund or something," Hayley said.

I thought about Marion's family. They could use the money too. "All I can say is that Bryce and I both agreed to look for the owner."

"Bryce too, huh?" Marion shook her head.

Woodland Park is a mountain town with lots of getaway cabins and bed-and-breakfasts. It had built up recently and changed a lot, but it still had that small-mountain-town feel to it.

"Right there," Sam said, pointing. A red sign said Quick Mart.

He parked and turned off his lights, and we watched the woman behind the register. She didn't look like I had pictured her. I don't know why, but I pictured her wispy, weighing as much as a French fry. I figured she'd be about 20 with weird hair, but this woman looked like she was in her 30s, heavyset, blondish hair. Dark eyelashes. A little too much makeup. We were too far away to tell if she wore any rings.

"What if I go in and make sure her name badge says Selena?" Marion said.

"Let's all go in together."

CHAPTER 75

Bryce

The final football challenge was tied in the fourth quarter, and we were laughing and having fun. Best party ever. Mom came in to check on us and watched a little of our game, but I think the noise got to her.

With the game on pause we got more to drink and took turns going to the bathroom.

Duncan had gone to Sam's little fridge for a refill and came running back. "I just heard something downstairs. Somebody moving around."

"I didn't know you were afraid of the dark," Chuck said.

"I'm serious," Duncan said, his teeth clenched.

"Probably Bryce's mom," Kael said.

"Let's check it out," I said.

I led the way, flipping on the light and carrying the heavy flashlight. Ashley and I keep our ATVs parked inside, plus there's a big freezer, a lawn mower, snowblower, and all of Sam's tools.

"Nobody here," Kael said. "Let's go back upstairs."

"What about under the stairs?" Chuck said.

There was an empty space there, dark and foreboding, big enough for someone to hide. I took the lead and aimed the flashlight inside. There were a few boxes there, but no one jumped out.

"Maybe some mice got a whiff of you and decided to move," Chuck said.

We all laughed and headed upstairs, but something caught my eye. Something white hung from the handlebar of my ATV. I found an envelope taped there. *Bryce* was printed on the front.

I looked around the barn again, sweeping every corner with my flashlight. Then I ran outside and did the same. I saw our dogs, Pippin and Frodo, at the back door, barking. Had they seen something?

Chuck snatched the envelope from me and held it to the light, trying to see inside. "I was right," he said.

"What?" I said.

"A love note from Marion." Everybody laughed but me. "It just says, 'Yes, I'll marry you.'"

I snatched the envelope back. "Very funny."

"He's probably right," Duncan said. "Did you see how she looked at you tonight? That girl is crazy in loooooove."

"You got the crazy part right," Kael said.

Suddenly this was becoming the worst party ever. I pulled out a single sheet of paper, folded three times.

Timberline,

Destroy this letter once you've read it and don't show it to anyone. Especially not your buddies upstairs.

Go to Red Rock Crossing between midnight and one, and you'll find all the evidence you need to help your friend. Just don't get me involved.

A friend

"What's it say?" Chuck said.

I wadded up the paper, stuffed it in my pocket, and looked at the clock. It was 11:45. "Nothing. You guys think you'll be all right without me for a little while?"

CHAPTER 76

✾ Ashley ✾

The Quick Mart was clean, for the most part. Hot dogs rolled in a glass case, nachos and cheese heating next to them. They also offered a new hot pumpkin drink, along with regular soft drinks and coffee. Hayley and Marion went for the pumpkin, Sam for the coffee.

Two guys with low-hanging jeans dug through their pockets, trying to come up with enough cash to pay for their bottles of Coors. When the cashier asked to see one guy's driver's license, he banged it on the counter and cursed.

Sam turned and looked at the guy, and he shut up.

"Help you?" the woman said. She wasn't wearing a name badge after all. I noticed several bruises on her arms.

"I'm looking for Selena," I said.

She raised her eyebrows. "That's me. What do you want?"

I explained how we'd found out about her, and Selena rolled her eyes. "Figures. He'd probably tell anybody who called where I am. What do you need?"

"Well, it's kind of complicated. We found something we think you might recognize. Can I show you?"

She looked at the others and squinted. "I guess. You guys aren't going to rob me, are you?"

I smiled. "Nothing like that."

I was holding the picture in front of me. When I turned it around, Selena's mouth dropped. "Where did you get that?"

"At a thrift store in Colorado Springs."

She took it and stared. "I got rid of all their stuff. I know they liked this a lot. Hung it in the hall outside my room."

"Do you remember it being in the will? Did they make a big deal about it?"

She frowned. "I was in kind of a daze back then, but now that you mention it, the will did say something about 'embracing it.' I figured they wanted me to become a Christian and all. Believe like they believed. But maybe they meant something else."

A man came in and bought a pack of cigarettes. We moved out of the way, and when he was gone, I stepped forward again. "We came from Red Rock to find you."

"All that way? Tonight?"

"It's my birthday party—mine and my brother's. When we found out where you were, my dad brought us."

"But why—?"

"We found something inside. A couple of things actually. We thought you'd want to have them."

"Inside?" She looked confused.

This is where it got tricky. Selena was low on money. If she got all we'd found would she blow it? Would her boyfriend or whoever was at her apartment spend it? I'd come this far and wasn't about to turn back.

"We found a packet of bills—money. A lot. Plus a map. We thought you could tell us what it was all about."

Selena nodded. "How much money?"

"Quite a bit," I said, hoping she wouldn't press me further.

She looked at the picture again. "You could have just kept it and not said anything."

I nodded. "I know. But my brother and I both thought, what if it had been our parents? What would we want someone else to do?"

"The Golden Rule." She chuckled and shook her head. "I may not have believed like them, but you can't help remembering. 'Do to others as you would like them to do to you.'" She looked at her watch. "I get off at eight tomorrow morning. Then I was going to get some sleep. I could probably drive there in the afternoon."

"Oh, it's Thanksgiving." I looked at Sam.

"You're welcome to join us," he said.

Selena smiled. "I won't bother your family, sir. But maybe I can clear up this whole map thing."

"We'll look for you tomorrow afternoon sometime," Sam said.

CHAPTER 77

Bryce

I didn't want to wake Mom, partly because she enjoys her sleep like other grown-ups and partly because I knew she would keep me home. I know it's not right to do something and ask forgiveness later, but I weighed the options and figured it was worth it if I got some information to help Boo.

I put my ATV in neutral and pushed it away from the barn, hopping on and coasting into the field. It wasn't until I was almost to town that I thought this might be a trap. Maybe somebody was trying to do the same thing to me that he or she had done to Boo.

I parked my ATV in the middle school parking lot and walked into town. Everything was quiet. Most houses were dark.

Something skittered across the road in the dull light of a streetlamp, and I stopped. Fox? Raccoon? I let it pass and kept walking, the red Closed sign at the Toot Toot Café ahead of me.

I held up across the street in the shadow of a flickering streetlamp. The thing buzzed like a bee, and I wished I could swat it.

In the distance came a low thumping and scraping, like metal against concrete. Then faint voices. I was about to cross the street when a car passed. I stayed out of sight until Officer Ormsby drove by and crossed the railroad tracks.

It was strange seeing the parking lot empty at Red Rock Crossing because it was always full during the day. The office-supply store had a Christmas display in its window with Santa opening a filing cabinet. Didn't make much sense, but it must have seemed Christmassy to the owners. A train whistle sounded, and the *chug-chug* of the 12:15 came rolling from the town north of us.

The blinds were closed at Carla's Cleaners, but I could see a sliver of light. I stepped onto the wooden sidewalk and it creaked. That sent my heart racing. I calmed down and heard the scraping sound again.

"Come on, hurry up!" someone said. A female.

"This thing is heavy," a guy said.

"Just help me get it into the back of the truck."

I crept onto the asphalt and followed the side of the building to the back. There I found a man helping Miss Sterling put barrels into a pickup.

"If you hadn't smashed your ATV, we wouldn't have to do this," Miss Sterling said.

"Don't rub it in. Those kids were too fast."

The guy looked familiar, but I couldn't place him.

"Ian said they were out at the dump yesterday and found the machine."

"They won't figure it out. Not in a million years. Besides, your contract with the new company starts next month. You'll be legal after this is gone."

They lifted a barrel onto the truck, and the bed dipped. I wondered how many more barrels they had.

"What about the Heckler kid?" Miss Sterling said.

The guy laughed. "That's the crazy thing. He confessed to the whole thing."

"Confessed?"

"I don't know why. Maybe he just wanted to be away from home. He's gonna get two years."

"Serves him right. He shouldn't have been snooping around up there."

I'd heard enough. I still had no idea what they were doing, but I did know that Boo was connected. I ran toward the street, then ducked around the other side of the Toot Toot and dialed the police station. It made a funny ring, and Officer Ormsby picked up, obviously still in his car.

I told him who and where I was, then asked if he could come quickly.

"I can head that way, but I'm kind of stuck right now," he said.

"Stuck?"

"I'm on the other side of the tracks, and a train's going through. What do you need?"

"There are people doing something wrong at Carla's."

"All right, as soon as this train is past, I'm there. Don't get too close, but watch which way they go, okay?"

"Yes, sir."

I tiptoed to the back of the Toot Toot, where I could get a good look at Carla's. Miss Sterling and her friend weren't there, but the truck was full of barrels. The train tracks ran just a few yards behind the drycleaners, so I wasn't worried about making too much noise. I inched closer, trying to get a good look. I was just about to the truck when someone headed out. I ducked behind the wheel and held my breath.

CHAPTER 78

Ashley

I was so excited about finding Selena that I knew I'd never sleep. I'd tried calling Sam's office phone, but no one answered. I had to wait until we got home to tell Bryce.

Sam went to the barn to get him. No way was I walking into that den of guys. Marion and Hayley crept up to my room and got ready for bed.

Sam came back a few minutes later. "The guys say Bryce took off almost an hour ago."

"Took off where?"

"They didn't know. He just said he had to leave. You check downstairs; I'll look up."

We searched the house but didn't find him. That's when I got an idea and checked the barn. "His ATV is gone!"

Sam scratched his chin. "Is there something going on you'd like to tell me about?"

"Just our investigation about Boo," I said.

Duncan walked down the stairs and waved at me. "I forgot to tell you. We heard something down here, and Bryce found a note taped to his ATV. That happened just before he left."

"Okay," Sam said. "You guys all right up there if we keep looking?"

"Sure. You want us to help?"

Sam looked at me.

"More eyes wouldn't hurt," I said.

We all piled into Sam's truck, me in front, the three guys in the back. I could tell they were trying to settle down, but it was hard after being cooped up in that room.

"Any idea where he might have gone?" Duncan said as we pulled out of the driveway.

"The dump?" I said.

"What would he be doing there?" Chuck said.

"Something we're working on."

"You try his cell phone yet?" Kael said. "Maybe he has it with him."

I hadn't thought of that and grabbed Sam's cell and dialed.

Bryce picked up before the second ring.

"Bryce? What's going on? Where are you?"

He didn't speak. I just heard a train *click-clacking*.

"Bryce?"

No answer. Just the train.

"He's near the train tracks," I said, keeping the phone close to my ear in case Bryce started talking.

"That could be anywhere in town," Duncan said.

"Wait! Red Rock Crossing! He's probably there, near the dry cleaners."

"He's getting his laundry done?" Chuck said.

The other two guys laughed, but Sam floored the accelerator and sped toward town.

CHAPTER 79

Bryce

When my phone rang, I was able to punch the green Answer button. I sat rigid against the truck, waiting for someone to discover me.

I pulled the phone to my ear as the train rumbled through and whispered, "Hello?"

"Bryce, where are you?" Ashley said.

"Red Rock Crossing—you guys home?"

"We're in the truck—"

"Have Sam get over here fast."

"On our way."

I hung up, then looked under the truck at the back door to Carla's. It was closed. Were they in the truck?

The train slowed, and the *click-clack* turned into a *c-l-i-c-k-c-l-a-c-k.*

"Who do we have here?" Miss Sterling said. I looked up and found her staring at me from the bed of the truck. "Steve! Looks like we have a visitor."

Steve, I thought. *The same Steve as at Spring Hill?*

"You said nobody would see us," Carla yelled. "Guess you were wrong. Again."

"Honest, there was nobody here when I pulled up."

I stood and held up my hands. Maybe I should have asked Mom if it was okay for me to go out on my ATV. "I was just cutting through here on my way back to the house," I said, my voice shaking. "I won't bother you. I'll just—"

"You won't bother us is right," Carla said. "Get him!"

I ran toward the train, but Steve was on me in seconds. I don't know why Ashley and I can never find slow criminals or ones who limp, but I guess that's our lot in life.

I fell to the ground, skinning my arm and scraping my face.

He pulled me up, held my arms behind me, and tossed my cell phone to Carla.

"Look, I don't even know what you guys are doing. Let me go."

"You know enough to tell the police to go up to the lake and have them snoop around," Carla said. "And you're trying to help that Heckler kid." She nodded toward the truck. "Put him in."

"What are we gonna—?"

"I said put him in!" she spat.

CHAPTER 80

⌘ Ashley ⌘

Sam flew toward town, and I could see the trail of dust in the moonlight. Moonlight dust. Kind of has a ring to it. The three guys in the back looked like they were on a roller-coaster ride, ready to whip their hands in the air and yell.

We hit the main paved road to town; then Sam veered left and took a dirt road I'd never been on before—and that's saying something because our town is really small. As it turned out, it was a fire-department access road, and it came out just a few streets from Red Rock Crossing.

"Check behind Carla's!" I said.

Sam whipped into the parking lot, but there was no one there. He zoomed to the back, but it was empty.

I saw something shiny on the asphalt ahead and got out. My heart raced as I picked up Bryce's smashed cell phone. "Bryce!" I shouted into the darkness.

No answer. Nothing but the squeak of train wheels on tracks. The thing was moving so slowly it made ants look like NASCAR racers. But the caboose wasn't far away.

I turned and spotted brake lights at the crossing, a couple of blocks away. I jumped back in the truck, and Sam floored it. Our tires squealed, and the truck's back end turned all the way around. The looks on the guys' faces behind me were priceless.

We sped onto the street. We scraped something and sparks flew.

"Wahoo!" Chuck yelled.

Sam screeched to a halt at the stop sign just as the caboose passed the crossing. There was an old truck with a bunch of barrels on it waiting to cross. I knew Bryce was in there.

Just as the caboose passed, lights came on and a siren blared on the other side of the tracks. White lights flashed at the back of the truck.

"He's backing up!" Kael said.

"Brace yourselves," Sam said.

Just as the truck got near, Sam pulled into the intersection, and the pickup smacked us in the front with a sickening crash. Two barrels toppled onto our hood and rolled to the ground.

Sam jumped out as the police officer slammed on his brakes. The officer pulled his pistol and yelled for the driver to get out.

Carla staggered and fell to the pavement. A guy jumped out the other side and started running, but Sam was on him in a flash.

I ran to the front, Kael, Chuck, and Duncan right behind me.

Bryce was slumped over in the front seat, holding his head in his hands.

"You all right, Timberline?" Duncan said.

Bryce was just milking it. He turned his head and smiled. I showed him his smashed cell phone, and he went over to Carla. "You're going to pay for this."

CHAPTER 81

Bryce

Officer Ormsby took my statement and said we could go home. Sam's truck still ran, though there was something leaking from the engine. He drove me to my ATV and let me ride it home. As soon as I got there I called Mr. Forster and told him what happened. He wasn't angry at us at all for waking him up.

Because of the excitement, we brought our stuff inside and slept downstairs. The girls all went to Ashley's room. Mom, Dylan, and Leigh slept through the whole thing.

I woke up to Chuck Burly's face two inches from mine. "Get up, Timberline. Police guy is here!"

I was still rubbing my eyes when I sat on the couch. Mom had poured Officer Ormsby a cup of coffee, and Sam was there too.

Does Sam ever sleep? I thought.

The girls had already left, and Mrs. Burly was there to pick up Chuck, Kael, and Duncan. She looked scared when she saw the officer.

"Come on, Mom," Chuck said. "We want to find out what happened."

"You get to the car, young man," Mrs. Burly said.

"I'll call you later," I yelled at the guys as they trudged to the car.

Officer Ormsby yawned and rubbed a hand over his face. "I went by Ian's house earlier, and he connected the dots. Carla paid him to frame Aaron."

"Why?"

"Seems he struck a deal with her, without his uncle knowing it, to store hazardous materials from the dry cleaners at the junkyard. Carla and Steve drove the materials back in the woods and dumped them."

"That's why we saw the dead animals," I said.

"Right. And if it had gone on much longer, it would have seeped into the water system. There are some stiff penalties for what they did."

"I didn't even know dry cleaners used chemicals," I said.

Officer Ormsby nodded. "And they have to pay a lot of money to get them disposed of properly. Carla thought she could get away with it, but she didn't count on crossing with you two."

"Did she admit she faked the robbery?" Ashley said.

"Not yet."

"How was Steve involved?" Sam said.

"He worked at Spring Hill and knew the Heckler kid from this summer. I guess he and Carla are sweethearts or something. Anyway, when they spotted Aaron at the lake, they hatched a plan to put him away and keep him there. This Steve guy had talked to Aaron about his hobbies—fixing up an old car."

"And that's how Ian knew to ask if he needed a part," I said.

"But Aaron didn't even know what was going on," Ashley said.

"I guess they didn't want to take any chances," Officer Ormsby said.

"Who left the note on Bryce's ATV?" Ashley said.

"I'll bet Ian can tell us about that too," I said. "Will Aaron get to come home?"

The officer put his hat on. "I'm not sure what will happen. But he owes you kids."

The doorbell rang, and Pippin and Frodo went crazy, like always. Mom answered it while we talked with the officer. A blonde lady walked inside.

Ashley jumped to her feet. "Selena!"

"I hope it's not too early, but I couldn't sleep," she said.

PART 9

SELENA

CHAPTER 82

⌘ Ashley ⌘

Mom got Selena some breakfast as we said good-bye to Officer Ormsby. Then Selena's story spilled out. She had met a guy when she was younger. Her parents didn't care for him and with good reason. She asked for money, and when they would only give her a little, she left. It kind of reminded me of the Prodigal Son.

She got word her parents had died, came back to take care of the property, and sold it to the first person who offered cash. When most of it ran out, the guy who had pledged his undying love took off with what was left.

"Is that the guy I talked to on the phone?" I said.

"No, but he's not much better. Everything I own is in the car out there. I'm hoping there will be enough money for me to make a new start. A few hundred dollars?"

Bryce looked at me and smiled. "I'll get the pouch."

A few minutes later he was back. I expected Selena to hover like a hungry hyena, looking at the pouch like some pot of gold at the end of the rainbow. Instead she took it and just stared at it.

"Why don't you open it?" I said.

"I was just thinking. You didn't have to find me. You could have just spent it on whatever you wanted, and no one would have ever known."

"*We* would have known," Bryce said.

Selena unzipped the pouch and peeked inside. She hadn't gotten past the 100s when I told her how much was there. Her mouth dropped; she looked inside again, then clutched the money to her chest and cried.

Mom handed her a box of tissues.

When she had calmed down, she told us how sorry she was for the way she'd treated her parents. "And I'll never get to tell them. I'll never be able to apologize."

I expected Mom to say something wise and motherly or maybe pull out some verse from the Bible.

Instead, it was Sam. "I expect they'd just be pleased that you're alive and want to turn things around," he said in his deep bass voice.

CHAPTER 83

Bryce

Sam drove Selena, Ashley, and me to Dynamite Peak and the property where the Willobys had lived. It was back in the woods—we would have never found it wandering around on our own.

We waited in the driveway while Selena talked with the owners. They said she could search wherever she wanted.

She took the map, wiping away tears as she studied the drawing her mom or dad had made. She got turned around once, then righted herself and came over a knoll at the back of the property.

"Dad used to come out here and make houses and forts with me," she said. "Then I got older and . . ."

She didn't talk for a long time—she just walked. I figured there were memories hanging around like tree branches. There are some trees other people can't climb for you. You have to do it yourself.

Sam had brought a shovel, but as it turned out, we didn't need it.

Selena looked into a tree and covered her mouth. "It must be in the tree house."

We climbed up with her, and she went straight to a shelf and pulled down a metal box.

"This was Dad's lockbox he kept in the upstairs closet," Selena said. "I always kidded him that—" she looked underneath, where a key was taped—"he never locked it, so it couldn't be a lockbox."

She put the key in, turned it, and opened it. Bugs crawled over paper and she lifted it, revealing a child's Bible. There was an envelope inside. A letter from her parents.

The three of us stepped back as she read it, tears flowing. I couldn't help getting a little choked up, but I wasn't about to cry.

She put the Bible back in the box and handed the letter to us. "After all you've done, you deserve to read this."

I held it and let Ashley and Sam read over my shoulder.

> Dearest Selena,
>
> We have prayed for you to come back for such a long time. I made this little shrine, a place where I could come and think of you and ask God to protect you. He may have given me the idea about the money in the painting. If you've found it, your mother and I are gone.
>
> Don't think we were ever angry at you. We have loved you since the day you were born, and we still believe in you. I always blamed myself for not loving you more, and I'm sure your mother felt the same.

This is the first Bible we bought you when you were small. I've highlighted some passages and left little notes for you. If you don't want to read it, I understand.

Selena, nothing you ever do could make us stop loving you. I hope you always remember that and that you'll accept the love that God offers. He loves you even more than your mother and I do, though I can't imagine that.

Bless you, my daughter.

All my love,
Dad

P.S. I'm glad you found the "unlocked box."

CHAPTER 84

Ashley

Selena stayed for Thanksgiving dinner. It felt appropriate that she be with a family on that day. Sam made Bryce help him clean the dishes, and they watched a football game while they did it. I showed Selena my room and a picture of my real dad. I told her the story as we sat on my bed and lit my favorite scented candle.

After we had pumpkin pie, Selena thanked us and started to leave.

"Why don't you stay?" Mom said. "You're not going back to Woodland Park, right?"

"No. Lease is up at the end of the month. I figured I'd stay in a hotel until I can find an apartment in the Springs. I have a lead on a job."

"We have a guest room," Mom said, choking up. "We'd be honored to have you stay with us while you look for a place."

"Stay! Stay!" Dylan chanted, hopping around Selena like she was a merry-go-round.

"I appreciate it," she said, "but you guys have done so much."

I wanted Mom to push, to make her stay, to say something else, but she didn't. "Well, if you ever need it, our house is yours."

Selena teared up again. "I might just take you up on that."

She gathered her things—the painting, some extra food Mom had packed, and her purse. She dug inside the zippered pouch and pulled out two $1,000 bills. "You both deserve more than this, I think."

"We couldn't," I said.

Bryce looked at me. "Why not?"

I elbowed him. "We're just happy you can use this to make a new start."

She put the bills back and pulled out two 100s. "I'd be grateful to know you at least got something for all the work you've done."

Before I could say anything, Bryce grabbed one of the bills. "We wouldn't want you to not be grateful on Thanksgiving."

We all laughed and waved as she drove out of sight.

Bryce and I just stood in the doorway, staring at our money.

A few minutes later a car pulled up, its headlights shining on our house. Someone got out and walked up to the porch. His arms hung at his sides, and he walked like some overgrown ape.

"Boo," I whispered.

He came to the top of the steps, his hands shoved into his pockets. "Hey."

"You're back," I said.

"Yeah. I guess the police explained things to the warden guy. And Mr. Forster must have known somebody down there."

"We're glad you're back," Bryce said.

"Yeah, me too." He looked back at the car, then at the porch. "Well, thanks."

"Have a good Thanksgiving," I said.

"Yeah, my dad's driving me. He said there was still some food left over at the house."

There was a long pause. I don't know whether it was the uncomfortable silence, the woodsmoke in the air, or the warm feelings I had from my birthday party and Selena, but something came over me and I did something I thought I would never do in a million years. I stepped forward and hugged Boo Heckler.

He didn't know what to do, I guess. From what Bryce said later, he looked like one of those store mannequins, his arms straight out. But Bryce said there was a hint of a smile on his face before he turned and walked back to his car.

About the Authors

Jerry B. Jenkins (jerryjenkins.com) is the writer of the Left Behind series. He owns the Jerry B. Jenkins Christian Writers Guild, an organization dedicated to mentoring aspiring authors. Former vice president for publishing for the Moody Bible Institute of Chicago, he also served many years as editor of *Moody* magazine and is now Moody's writer-at-large.

His writing has appeared in publications as varied as *Reader's Digest, Parade, Guideposts,* in-flight magazines, and dozens of other periodicals. Jenkins's biographies include books with Billy Graham, Hank Aaron, Bill Gaither, Luis Palau, Walter Payton, Orel Hershiser, and Nolan Ryan, among many others. His books appear regularly on the *New York Times, USA Today, Wall Street Journal,* and *Publishers Weekly* best seller lists.

Jerry is also the writer of the nationally syndicated sports story comic strip *Gil Thorp,* distributed to newspapers across the United States by Tribune Media Services.

Jerry and his wife, Dianna, live in Colorado and have three grown sons and three grandchildren.

Chris Fabry is a writer and broadcaster who lives in Colorado. He has written more than 40 books, including collaboration on the Left Behind: The Kids series.

You may have heard his voice on Focus on the Family, Moody Broadcasting, or Love Worth Finding. He has also written for Adventures in Odyssey and Radio Theatre.

Chris is a graduate of the W. Page Pitt School of Journalism at Marshall University in Huntington, West Virginia. He and his wife, Andrea, have been married 27 years and have nine children, two dogs, and one cat.